THE LOST *HĀDĪTH*

S. Milsap Thorpe

Published by Rogue Phoenix Press
Copyright © 2014

Names, characters and incidents depicted in this book are products of the author's imagination or are used fictitiously. Any resemblance to actual events, locales, organizations, or persons, living or dead, is entirely coincidental and beyond the intent of the author or the publisher. No part of this book may be reproduced or transmitted in any form or by any means, electronic or mechanical, including photocopying, recording, or by any information storage and retrieval system, without permission in writing from the publisher.

ISBN: 978-1534745254

Credits
Cover Artist: Designs by Ms. G
Editor: Christie L. Kraemer

Dedication

A'isha and the women of the world.

Prologue

Arabia, after Hijra or about 627, Anno Domini

A slender young woman wearing a long, black *abaya* and an attached *ḥijāb* below her chin, searched for something near the base of a date palm as the hot Arabian sun rose in the east and warmed the desert sand beneath her feet.

Frustrated, she removed her *ḥijāb*, held it in her hand and overturned some small rocks searching under them. Finding nothing, she stood and surveyed the desolate dunes surrounding her. Her dark, intense brown eyes surveyed the landscape as the sun illuminated her olive complexion. A mild wind fluttered her long, black, shiny hair, wrapping around her stunning, Arabic face. She licked her lips to moisten them, walked down a path and around the edge of a dune.

Nearing an outcrop in the hillside, she spotted another date palm. *Could this be the one?* She knelt down and searched at its base. There it was. Relieved, she grabbed the necklace, its *Zifar*, Yemenite beads, partly black and partly white. She put it around her neck.

During her frantic search, she had lost track of time. Cresting a large rocky knoll, she descended and found her camp at the base of the dune struck. Only markings in the sand where tents pitched earlier remained. The wind, blowing the sand around, made the markings indistinguishable.

She sat and rested near where her tent had been under a *ghaf* tree, its large and evergreen canopy affording her much needed shade. She figured when her servants noticed her absence they would return for her. They must have lifted her *howdah*, and thought, because she was so light, comparable to many young women of her age she must have been in it.

Sleep overcame her.

An hour later a man approached, stopped and steadied his camel upon seeing the young woman. The man, Safwan ibn al-Muattal, saw her face and looked away out of respect. He recognized her because he had known her face before the order for compulsory veiling.

He waited until she awoke and saw him there on his camel. He continued to look away from her as she reattached her *ḥijāb* and veiled her face. He recited his *Istirja*,' "*Inna lillahi wa inna llaihi raji'un,*" *truly to Allah we belong and truly to him we shall return.* He dismounted his camel and made it kneel, putting his foot on its front legs.

She climbed upon the camel and rode while he walked at its side holding the reins. At no time did either speak to the other. Two hours passed trekking across the desert landscape until they caught up with the caravan while it halted for a rest in the hot midday sun.

She rejoined her servants.

Not long after the event rumors spread that she and the man who had rescued her had engaged in an affair. This event would cause great embarrassment to all concerned and create a crisis in her marriage and her husband's fragile ministry. Eventually her husband backed her accounting after he received a revelation.

Arabia, after Hijra, or 660 AD

The woman rode on a camel into a small, ancient village. A young manservant walked beside it holding the reins. She ate Arabian palm dates he bought from a man selling them aside the road. She lifted her veil slightly to allow herself to eat.

When she finished her dates, he replenished their water pouches. They rested for a few minutes before continuing on their journey.

They came upon a large and elongated sandstone mountain. He led on as far as he could until the path narrowed at the base of the mountain. He helped her down from the camel. She waited while he untied a tall pottery jar from the back of the camel and placed it on the ground. He untied four codices, wrapped in linens and handed them to her.

Despite being in her late forties, she was still quite attractive. She led the way up the side of the mountain as he followed holding the pottery jar. The codices she carried were new; their sturdy covers made of thin wooden strips coated in wax with the pages inside consisting of a heavy parchment made of sheepskin.

They rounded a large rock and saw petroglyphs; the largest called the Lion of *Shuwaymus* etched into the rocks there. All around *Shuwaymus* they saw hundreds of engravings marking the sandstone. They continued and passed many images chiseled into the sandstone including ones of cheetah, hyenas, dogs, cattle, oryx, ibex and horses. They rounded a protrusion and saw more images, this time of mules, camels, ostriches, humans, and serpentines.

Down the path, they climbed over rocks, through small passageways, around boulders and deeper into the mountain where they rounded a bend in the path and came upon some cotton shrubbery. She moved the shrubbery aside with the back of her hand and pointed at an opening to a small cave. "Here," she said.

He opened the pottery jar and she placed the codices inside. She watched as he held the jar out in front of him and crawled into the small cave.

The cave went back into the hillside by several yards. He inched into a chamber and placed the jar on a ledge. He shimmed backwards out of the cave and brushed the sand from his long white garment, his *Thobe*.

She surveyed the area and drew a map of the location on a parchment. They walked back down the path and returned to the village.

Chapter One

    An American F-16 Falcon cruised over Baghdad early this morning. While the city slept, the jet streaked across the so-called Green-zone, the fortified seat of the Iraqi government and the heart of American operations. It circled the central city and released its payload, a 2000 pound, GPS-guided smart bomb. The F-16 banked hard and disappeared over the horizon.

    The bomb found its way to the target, a house on Haifa Street in a residential area of Baghdad. The area consisted of estates, many belonging to former Baathist members of Saddam Hussein's government. The area also had abject poverty; this was a neighborhood of the haves and the have nots.

    The house exploded into a fireball, smoke billowing into the sky and debris rained down throughout the neighborhood.

    As the house burned, the blood-red sun rose. A few minutes after the debris from the blast had settled, American soldiers rushed in to secure the area. Setting up a perimeter with their Humvees, they cordoned off the street. A few brave and curious civilians ventured out of their homes to investigate. Most of the locals disappeared back into their houses when they discovered the Americans out in force.

    The house burned. A ragtag Iraqi fire unit arrived on scene a few minutes later and within an hour had the fire out.

    The soldiers surveyed the wreckage, walking through the ruins of the house. They searched for several minutes and found no signs of life, or anything of intelligence value.

"Let's clear out," said Captain Bryce. "Sergeant, call it in."

"Yes, sir," said Sergeant Maines. "Load up. We're moving out," he said to the soldiers lingering there. The soldiers made their way to their Humvees.

Private Randall, near the rear of the group, bent down and picked up a round and flat, bronze-colored disk, the size of a golf ball. A beaded necklace, partly black and partly white, slid back and forth through an opening near the pendant's edge. He squirted water from his Camelbak over it, wiping it clean. He noticed the disk had Arabic writing on one side and some engravings on the other.

"Whaddaya got, Randall?" Maines said.

"A souvenir, Sergeant."

"Awright, awright, let's go."

Randall hung the necklace around his neck and stuffed the pendant down the front of his ACUs. He jogged over to his Humvee and jumped in. The soldiers moved out.

Chapter Two

    The Baghdad heat was brutal on the human body and patrolling the dusty Sadr City neighborhoods in full combat gear taxed the best. Today was no exception as a platoon on foot patrol entered a marketplace at eleven hundred hours and snaked its way through the crowd.
    Private Johnson noticed a young Iraqi, seventeen years old, wearing an oversized *Dishdasha*, an Iraqi robe, dart out from between two buildings. The boy sprinted across the street toward a group of shoppers gathered near a vegetable cart and headed for the platoon. Johnson used hand signals to alert Sergeant Patrick Burns on the other side of the street.
    Burns saw the boy and shouted to his platoon, "Take cover. Suicider at one o'clock." He then yelled in Arabic, "Everyone, take cover. He's got a bomb."
    The boy heard the warning as well, because he tore off his *Dishdasha*. Underneath, strapped to his body like a scuba diver's Buoyancy Compensator, was a suicide vest. He held his thumb on a devise wired to the bomb vest.
    The civilians screamed and ran in all directions. The platoon took cover behind cars, two soldiers ducked in an alley, and Burns jumped and rolled behind a truck. He tried to sight his rifle on the boy, but couldn't do it fast enough as the boy yelled, "*Allah Akhbar*!" and blew himself up.
    The shock wave blew past the huddled platoon.
    After the dust and debris had settled, Burns and his platoon fanned out and took up defensive positions around the market. The scene was

eerily quiet, mostly due to everyone's ringing ears. Smoke from the bomb billowed high above and civilian survivors walked around in bewilderment.

Burns hustled around the scene making sure his soldiers were okay and had secured the area. "Call it in, Smith," he said to his radioman.

Smith reported into his radio: "Alpha, zero two niner. This is delta four four zero. Suicider in sector mike, four two. Request Iraqi medical personnel for civilian causalities."

A few minutes later, after the platoon had triaged the wounded, Burns walked back over to the truck he had hid behind during the blast. His medic reported to him, "All civilians, Sergeant. Fifteen dead, twenty wounded."

Burns nodded and sighed. The medic went back to assist with the wounded.

Burns dug a fat cigar out of his shirt pocket, but didn't light it. He put it in his mouth and surveyed the devastation. A scene such as this didn't get any easier the second, third, or fourth time. At six feet and forty-eight years of age, Burns was in exceptional physical shape. He watched as civilians tried to find loved ones or tend to the injured.

A couple minutes later, Lieutenant Sharon Fischer pulled up in a Humvee and parked beside Burns, her military police platoon following. "Jesus, Burns," she said. "What a mess." She jumped out and examined the scene.

"Yes, ma'am, it certainly is." He stuck his cigar back into his mouth, wanting so badly to light it.

She slurped some water from her Camelbak and said, "The Iraqi's should be on-scene shortly. What's the count?"

"Fifteen dead, twenty wounded."

"Specialist Olmedo," she hollered to her medic nearby in a Humvee, "See what you can do for the wounded."

"Yes, Ma'am." Olmedo jumped out and hustled around the scene assisting.

"You injured, Sergeant?" she said to Burns. "You've got something bloody on your left cheek." She motioned to her own cheek where the smudge was on his.

"I don't think so." He wiped his cheek with his fingertips, but failed to find the spot.

"Here," she said, taking a tissue from her pocket and wiping at his cheek. It wiped off clean, leaving not a trace of an injury. She studied the gob in her tissue. "It's flesh." She tossed the tissue on the ground near her feet then unfolded a laminated field map she pulled from her map case. "We're here, as you know. We have to push on up this street."

His mind elsewhere, he rolled his cigar around in his mouth and watched as she used her finger and traced the route on the map.

An Iraqi security force and medical team finally arrived on scene. Fischer's platoon moved out and Burns gathered his platoon and moved on, pushing up the deserted street. Fortunately, there were no other dramatic events this day. While Burns and his platoon walked the streets of Baghdad, his mind wandered.

Fifteen years earlier, Patrick Burns walked across the *Pont d'Lena* in Paris, France holding the hand of an attractive woman on one side and a young child on the other. "There it is," he said.

"*Pardon*," the woman said to two tourists standing there on the bridge. "*Pourriez vous prenez une photo de nous?*"

"Sorry," the man said. "We don't speak French."

"Americans?" she said with an Arabic accent.

"Canadians, actually."

"Oh, could you please take a photo of us?"

"Sure." The man took the camera from her.

Burns, the woman, and the young girl posed on the bridge, the Eiffel tower in the background. He held on to the woman tightly with one arm and the young girl with the other. They smiled for the camera.

Hand-in-hand they made their way over to the tower and boarded the elevator, riding it to the top. On the upper deck, as the Paris wind blew the woman's shiny, long, black hair across her face, Burns surveyed the grand city before them. He hugged and kissed the woman. The girl, the spitting image of the woman, glanced over.

"Daddy," she said, teasing.

"You're not jealous of Mommy are you?" He picked her up, swung her around, and hugged her too, planting an exaggerated kiss on her cheek.

"Now I am jealous," the woman said.

Burns snapped out of his daydream as he and his platoon entered their base camp on the outskirts of Baghdad.

Chapter Three

A robed, bearded man stood near the door to a dimly lit, windowless basement room, a single light bulb hanging above him. He watched as two young men stood over an old and frail Iraqi man who bled from his nose, his ears and mouth on the cold cement floor.

"Please, as Allah is my witness," the old man said in Arabic through the tears streaming down his face. He held his hands as if he prayed.

One of the young men pointed his AK-47 at the old man's forehead. The other young man, without a rifle, kicked the old man in the stomach. The old man screamed and coughed up blood.

The man holding the rifle turned and peered over his shoulder at the robed man. The robed man, Hasan Ali al-Salah, appeared older than his thirty-six years, due to the stress of always having to be on-guard for his safety. He has had many sleepless nights these past few years as warring factions plied for power in war-torn Iraq. Before that, he even had to be on-guard during Saddam Hussein's time because *Shiites* were not in favor.

He moved and stood over the old man. "Lift him," he said. The young men held the old man up by his armpits. The old man couldn't stand or kneel on his own, so they dangled him on his knees. "We have searched long and hard," said al-Salah. "We have only now learned that you know the whereabouts of the keeper of the lost necklace."

The old man's head hung low so al-Salah motioned to one of his henchman to lift his head. "We do not wish to harm you. We only seek the necklace."

"I know nothing of a keeper of a necklace," the old man managed to say after coughing up blood.

Al-Salah sighed and nodded to his associate who held the rifle.

Using the butt of the rifle, the young man smashed the old man in the teeth. He screamed and bloody teeth fell from his mouth.

The old man cried, cupped his hands together and tried to reach out to al-Salah, but one of al-Salah's goons twisted the old man's left arm behind his back. He again screamed.

"We know you work for this man," al-Salah said. "You are referred to as the chief servant. The chief servant knows everything about his master's home. This master you served was rumored to be the keeper of the lost necklace. You have more than once talked of this to others."

"Please, please. Praise be to Allah, the compassionate, the merciful." The old man's head drooped low again.

"Our sources have told us that you have referred to your master as the keeper of the lost necklace."

The old man did not answer, only cried.

"Your life will be spared if you tell us this fact," al-Salah said, his dark, cold eyes narrowing as he circled him.

The old man still did not answer. Al-Salah nodded to his torturer. He again raised the butt of the rifle.

"Wait," the old man said. "Praise be to Allah." Through his tears, swollen and bloody face, he struggled to get the words out. "I had heard others... Yes...dressed like you...other holy men...they came to see him." He paused to catch his breath. "They called him the keeper, yes. But I knew not what this meant. By the blessed Muhammad, may peace be upon him, I am telling you the truth." He whimpered.

"Who is this man?"

The old man sniffled and looked up. Al-Salah's beady little eyes bore into him. "It will be easier on you, my friend," al-Salah said, "if you confess to Allah."

Sniffling, he said, "This man you seek called the keeper is dead. His house was destroyed by the American infidels."

"When?"

"Two days ago they bombed his house."

"So, it was indeed Jabber Hassef?"

"Yes."

Al-Salah thought a moment, adjusting his *Amamah*, the black imam hat, and slinked back over to the other side of the small room. Facing away from the old man, he said, "It was rumored that a pendant was attached to the necklace, bronze it was. Is this true?"

The old man hesitated, but when he saw al-Salah's thug raise the rifle butt at him again, he said, "Yes. I did see it once. An imam came to see him. He showed it to the imam to prove he had it."

"Could you see the markings?"

"No, I could not, but I had heard Hassef say the necklace belonged to the Mother of the Believers."

Al-Salah spun around to face the old man. "You are certain of this?"

"Yes."

Al-Salah moved closer and leaned over the old man. "Where in the house was the necklace kept?"

"I do not know. Hassef kept it hidden and had said to the imams and others he took money from that the pendant would vindicate A'isha."

Al-Salah's hooligans perked up.

"The Americans went through everything," continued the old man. "I know Hassef was there at the time the house was bombed and is now dead. But I do not know of where this necklace is."

"You have done well, Zamin al-Hayali. Allah will praise you." He nodded to the henchman holding the rifle, turned, and departed the room, closing the door behind him.

"Please," al-Hayali said. "Please, I have a family."

The man holding the rifle plugged al-Hayali with one shot, splattering his brains out the back of his head and onto the wall.

Chapter Four

Sergeant Maines entered the barracks where his platoon rested. He wandered over to Private Randall's cot where Randall snored away in peaceful bliss amongst a dozen slumbering soldiers.

Maines kicked the base of Randall's cot. "Wake up, Randall."

Randall jolted out of his slumber. "What's up, Sergeant?"

"Captain wants to see you about that necklace you found."

"Now?"

"Now. You can go as is. Bring the necklace."

Randall sat up and slipped his boots on, the pendant swinging around his neck. Rubbing his tired eyes, in a brown T-Shirt and boxers, he followed Maines to the captain's office in a small building not far away. Maines knocked on the doorframe to the captain's office because the door was already open.

"Captain?"

"Come in, Sergeant."

Maines entered followed by Randall. Captain Bryce stood and walked out from behind his desk. "Private Randall."

"Sir," Randall said, coming to attention.

"At ease. This is Major Cunningham."

Cunningham, a thirty-year-old African-American man wearing immaculately pressed ACUs, stepped forward from the side of Bryce's desk. Randall assumed the position of attention again.

"At ease," Cunningham said. "You understand you can't keep the necklace, Private?"

"Yes, I figured, sir."

"It may be an antiquity and belongs to the Iraqi people."

Randall nodded, lifted the necklace off over his head and handed it to him.

Cunningham glanced at the necklace and the markings on the pendant then put it in his leather briefcase. "It's important that you did find it in the rubble of that house, Randall. Now it will find its rightful place in an Iraqi museum."

"Yes, sir."

"Very well," Cunningham said. "Captain?"

"Thank you, Randall. You're dismissed."

Randall came to attention, turned on a military dime, and departed, followed by Maines.

Chapter Five

Al-Salah climbed out of his armored-plated Lexus SUV. Black-masked security guards, gripping AK-47s, quickly surrounded their leader and escorted him into a heavily fortified private palatial estate in the Sadr City area of Baghdad. The American military and Iraqi forces had yet to rein him in and to control the area because of the militia he controlled, his army of *anbiyaa*, prophets. American and Iraqi authorities feared bloody battles if they were to make a move, so negotiations continued between the Iraqi government, the Americans and al-Salah's forces.

Al-Salah walked up the sidewalk to his compound as carefully staged followers knelt down before him and praised him as he passed. He waved his hand over them. A man shouldering a video camera recorded the spectacle.

Inside his extravagant manor, al-Salah hurried into a meeting room where his seven lieutenants sat waiting. They stood, bowed and kissed his hand as he filed past them. The room was large and opulent in Arabic woodwork, tile, rugs and paintings. Everyone sat in the middle of the room on ornate chairs. Al-Salah had to rearrange his *aba*, a large black and expensive hand-made robe made in *Najaf*, in order to sit. All were well dressed in traditional Iraqi garments.

Al-Salah began, "I have the news we have long waited for." He paused to gauge their anxious faces. "The lost necklace we seek is within our grasp."

The men stirred, many gasping.

"The *Sunni* Jabar Hassef had possession of it."

An older, sun-parched man, inquired, the index finger on his left hand shaking as he raised it, "The Incidence of the Necklace? The one that belonged to A'isha?"

Another old cleric said in a whisper, "The one said to contain clues as to the whereabouts of the lost collection of *ahādīth*?"

"It is not certain at this time whether this is all still but a myth, an elaborate hoax," al-Salah said, "however, I have forces at work to retrieve the necklace so we can be sure." He paused and looked away.

"What is it?" another bearded man said.

"My sources inform me the Americans may have possession of the necklace."

"Blasphemous," said one of the men.

"We shall declare a *fatwā* upon them until they return it to its lawful owners," said another.

"No, not at this time," al-Salah said raising his hand. "We have operatives working within the government who can inquire as to its whereabouts. I suspect the Americans do not know what they have, and will turn it over to the government for placement in a museum. We will take possession of it then."

"Master," said yet another of his supporters, scratching his untidy beard, "I know we have all heard of this rumor, but can we be certain this *hādīth* exists and is a true component of the *Sunnah*, or is this more trickery on behalf of our *Sunni* brothers?"

"I know of your concern, Muhammad al-Mussawi. However, I am assured by many *ulema* that this *hādīth* did exist at one time, and was rumored to have been hidden by A'isha since the time of Abu Bakr. We must take possession and destroy it once and for all because it is believed to be harmful to our *Shiite* brothers." He scanned their weary, uncertain faces. "This necklace and the mysteries it may lead to have blackmailed our faithful brothers for a thousand years." He clenched his fist in the air. "As you know, dubious men have become rich because of this. Some argue this *hādīth* contains important transcriptions directly from the *sahabah*, most likely attributed to A'isha herself." He paused to weigh their reactions. Most nodded, some grunted.

Al-Mussawi stroked his beard and said, "I will provide all at my disposal in your search for the necklace. I have a network of spies at your command."

"Thank you, my brother." Al-Salah stood, the men standing and bowing as he passed and left the room.

Al-Salah retired for the day to his garden, sitting in an oversized chair. He put his feet up on a stool to allow a manservant to wash and massage his feet while another manservant fanned him with a large palm frond. Yet another man served him a home-cooked meal of *Pacha*, a delicious, slowly cooked blend of sheep's head, stomach and feet, bubbling in a broth. He enjoyed a mixed side dish of pickled vegetables, *turshi*.

Chapter Six

A black GMC Suburban wound its way through the streets of Baghdad, Major Eugene Cunningham sat in the backseat reading a file on Hasan Ali al-Salah. Cunningham was just handed intelligence that al-Salah had been actively pursuing the necklace for some time. Although he knew of al-Salah, he wanted to refresh his understanding of him.

He flipped a page in the file and read how Hasan Ali al-Salah was the third son of Imam Muhammad Ali al-Salah. The father had been a highly influential and respected imam who claimed to be a direct descendant of the Prophet Muhammad, as many imams in the *Shiite* branch of Islam professed.

The elder al-Salah and Hasan's two older brothers, Cunningham learned, were murdered by Saddam Hussein's secret police after the Gulf War. Saddam, a *Sunni*, representing the minority *Sunnis* in Iraq, had long suppressed the *Shiite* majority. The elder al-Salah and his first two sons had been a constant threat to Saddam's rule. Saddam tolerated them for the longest time, but when *Shiite* clerics began to challenge Saddam's regime after the Gulf War, Saddam had them arrested and shot. Their bodies were never found.

Hasan Ali al-Salah was a young man at the time of his father and brothers' disappearance, and was considered harmless. He had fled to Iran after the war when Saddam punished the *Shiites* after their uprising. When coalition forces withdrew from southern Iraq, Saddam killed thousands, some said hundreds of thousands. Hasan Ali al-Salah held American

President George Herbert Walker Bush responsible.

Cunningham continued reading the file as his SUV approached the Green-Zone. He read how many in the *Shiite* community in Iraq, particularly the Grand Ayatollah, did not approve of Hasan Ali al-Salah's influence and role in the war-torn country. They considered him not to be in equal stature as was his father. He had not the formal schooling that was required for an imam. He was not an imam, but he dressed and acted the part.

Cunningham closed the file and placed it in his briefcase. He exited the SUV at the main entrance to the Green Zone and entered through its multi-layered checkpoints. His credentials thoroughly checked, his body searched, briefcase examined, he was allowed to pass. He went into the military's governmental liaison offices.

When Cunningham entered his small, windowless office, he saw Colonel James Graves sitting there waiting inside the door reading briefing papers. Graves was in his early fifties, shaved head, medium in stature, and had neatly pressed ACUs. He could pass as G. Gordon Liddy's twin. "Colonel," said Cunningham.

"Major," Graves said shuffling his papers and putting them back into his briefcase. He stood and moved over in front of Cunningham's desk.

"Please, sit, Colonel," Cunningham said.

Graves sat in the guest chair. Cunningham pulled the necklace and attached pendant from his briefcase and handed it to Graves. "You sure it's the one?" Graves said, turning the pendant over to scan the side containing the engravings.

"Absolutely," said Cunningham sitting in the chair behind his desk. "My sources confirm it is and that everyone has been looking for it for over a thousand years. Al-Salah wants it. So too does Yassim and the Brotherhood of Bakr."

"Then there's no way we can hand it over if it does indeed lead to these writings."

"I agree." Cunningham took the pendant back from Graves.

Graves leaned in closer and spoke softly, "I want this kept within the company, Gene." He sat back in the chair again. "This Professor Patrick Burns with the California Guard?"

"Yes."

"You know of him?"

"Every detail," Cunningham said. He stood up and opened his filing cabinet. He fingered through a few files, pulled one out and handed it to Graves. "He's cleared. Not a blemish."

Graves opened and scanned the file on Burns. "Yeah, but what about his baggage?"

"Well," Cunningham said, "the record says it was hard on him at first, but his professorship and the Guard kept him busy. His daughter too." He sat back down in his chair. "He's an expert on this and, because of his military skill, I think we can trust him more." Cunningham put the necklace back into his briefcase. "I don't think he'll be a problem."

"How was that possible in the first place?" Graves said. "I mean, his wife never converted?"

"Yeah, but it happens all the time. Look at my wife. She's Jewish. Can you really imagine? A black Baptist from Georgia marrying a white Jew from New York City, a government lawyer at that?"

"More cosmopolitan these days, if you ask me. But a Catholic and a Muslim? The Crusades and all that?"

"Could you image a Jew and a Muslim? I've heard in Israel it happens and breaks apart families. Anyway, I think Burns and his wife were both more agnostics than anything."

"But a professor and the military? How rare is that?"

"Not all college professors are liberal, radical anti-military, Jim."

Graves raised his left eyebrow. He handed the file on Burns back to Cunningham, stood and scanned the maps of Iraq and the Middle East on Cunningham's wall. "Okay. I'll leave it in your hands. Brief me at least once a week, sooner if events unfold." He turned and faced Cunningham. "I don't want this on the DCI's desk yet," he said. "If at all. I think if these writings turn out to be of any value, this whole thing could blowup and turn into an international incident and I want him and POTUS to have plausible deniability."

"Understood, Colonel."

Graves turned and left the office. Cunningham opened and scanned Burns' file. On his second tour of duty in Iraq with the California National Guard, he was a rarity amongst non-commissioned officers. In the civilian world Burns was an assistant professor of philosophy and religious studies at the Claremont-McKenna College in Claremont, California. His specialties included the origins of Christianity and Islam, and the resultant battles for the holy land. In fact, his last book was *The Jews, Christians and Muslims: Why the Holy Land will never rest.*

Cunningham learned how Burns had worked his way through San Francisco State University in the late nineteen eighties and had majored in Middle Eastern and Islamic Studies. He stayed in the Guard and while many of his Guard superiors over the years recommended he seek a commission, he turned it down, preferring to train and lead young soldiers. He said the Non-Commissioned Officer, NCO, was the most important member of the military who directly affected young soldiers, similar to a professor and his students. Cunningham read how Burns' National Guard service didn't sit well with his colleagues. Although they admired his commitment to his county and the young soldiers under his charge, they were not pleased about this war, or his absence from the college. As a professor, Burns could easily plan around his college schedule and fit in the Guard's training sessions. The war he could not.

Cunningham closed the file and stuffed it in his briefcase. He departed his office and hurried down a corridor and through a labyrinth of hallways past many offices. An operation such as this, the so-called occupation of Iraq, was a massive, bureaucratic endeavor. He entered a large office and stood in front of a receptionist's desk. "I'm here to see Colonel Mack."

"He's in the DFAC," the sergeant said.

"Thank you, Sergeant." He departed the office and descended the stairs at the end of the hallway. He traversed another hallway until he came to the dining facility where dozens of soldiers and civilian workers dined.

Cunningham scanned the DFAC and spotted Colonel Mack, a gray-haired man in his fifties. His face drawn and wrinkled, he seemed to be enjoying his chicken sandwich and fries while he scanned the military's signature newspaper, the *Stars and Stripes*. Cunningham walked up and stood next to him. "That stuff will kill you, Colonel," Cunningham said.

"The fries?" Mack said. "Yeah, well, everything eventually kills you. Have a seat, Major." Cunningham slipped into the chair opposite Mack. Mack lifted his napkin from his lap and dabbed his lips. "Whaddaya have for me?"

"A Sergeant Burns in the California Guard." Cunningham passed Mack the file folder from his briefcase.

Mack opened it and scanned the information. "Sergeant Burns. I think I've heard of him. He's some sort of professor. What for?" Mack glanced up at Cunningham.

Cunningham smiled back at him. Mack read the message loud and clear. "I get it," Mack said, scanning the file and flipping over a page to inspect the next one. "Well, he's a rare bird." He read from the file: "A professor of early Christian and Islamic studies?" Mack scrutinized Graves again. "You're kidding?"

Unbeknownst to Cunningham and Mack, an Iraqi boy in his early twenties bussing the table next to them listened in on the conversation. He had dirty hands from cleaning tables and dishes, and he wiped the table with a rag.

"Must be an important mission," Mack continued. He handed the file back to Cunningham.

Cunningham put the file in his briefcase and stood to go. "I need him released for this mission ASAP. This comes from the top."

"Okay," Mack said. "I'll have the papers drawn up after I finish my lunch."

"Thanks, Colonel."

Mack went back to his meal as Cunningham rushed off.

The Iraqi bussing the table watched Cunningham zip across the DFAC for the door on the far side of the room. He picked up a food tray and his cleaning cloth and followed.

He kept his distance as Cunningham traced his steps back to his office. The Iraqi looked over his shoulder several times to ensure no one had followed him. He saw Cunningham enter his office and close the door behind him. The Iraqi slowly strode past the office, noting the number 27b on the door. He then ambled off down the corridor.

Chapter Seven

The woman with Burns in Paris, dressed in an *abaya* with a *ḥijāb* covering her head, entered the King Fahad hospital in *Medina*, Saudi Arabia. A veil masked her face and only a slit for her eyes allowed her to see.

She found her way up to the third floor and spoke to an attendant who pointed to a room down the hall. She nodded and headed that way.

Entering the hospital room, she stopped in her tracks upon seeing a frail, ashen and weak woman lying on a bed. She removed her *ḥijāb* and veil, her long, black and shiny hair falling loose. Her stunning Arabic face was dark olive in complexion and skin smooth as silk.

The sick woman in the bed smiled as the woman approached and bent over to kiss her forehead. The sick woman in the bed raised her hand, stroked the woman's face and said, "I have missed you so dearly for so long."

Tears welled up in the other woman's eyes. "Yes. And I have missed you so very much, sister." She pulled up a chair and sat beside her sister, holding her hand.

"How are your husband and beautiful daughter?"

"They are very well, Nafi'a."

"I am so happy for you, Fatima," Nafi'a said. "You have done so well and I am so proud of you."

Fatima smiled and wiped a tear from her cheek. "How is Mother?"

"She is secretly very proud of you too. The successful American she calls you."

"And Papa?"

Nafi'a lost her smile and closed her eyes. "He has forbidden anyone to speak your name." She opened her eyes and gazed up. "Papa caught Mother with one of your photographs, the one with young Sara. He ripped it up and beat her for it."

"I am so sorry, Nafi'a."

"No, don't be. Mother took it as a badge of honor."

Tears streamed from Fatima's eyes, and she leaned forward, placing her head on her sister's chest.

Nafi'a stroked Fatima's hair. "I am not afraid, Fatima. I have lived an honorable life according to Allah's good grace. I am at peace. I am so happy that you are loved and have found all you ever wanted."

Fatima sniffled.

"Has Patrick come with you?" Nafi'a said, perking up a little.

Fatima raised her head and said, "No. No, he could not make it. But he sends his love." She wiped a tear away.

Fatima stayed with her dying sister for a few hours talking about their childhood together, their parents, and her life in America.

Sergeant Burns snapped out of his daydream when Private Scott Grant said in a squeaky, southern drawl, "I don't get it, Sergeant."

"Get what?" Burns said, staring at a book he was trying to read.

"I mean, aren't they all Muslims?"

"What're you talking about?" He closed his book.

"*Sunnis* and *Shiites*."

"*Sunnis* and *Shiites*?" Burns shifted in his seat.

"Yes, *Sunnis* and *Shiites*. I mean, they're all Muslims, aren't they? Why do they fight each other?"

"What's your denomination?" Burns lifted his feet up onto the adjacent sofa.

"My denomi...what?"

"What persuasion of Christianity do you subscribe to?"

"Do I subscribe to? You talk too much like a professor, Sergeant. I'm Christian, of course."

Burns and his platoon rested this night in a common area where they read, played cards, or sat and listened to music on their iPods. Several soldiers waited in line for telephones and computer terminals to contact their loved ones back in the states.

"Well, there are Baptists, Episcopalians, Mormons, Quakers, Methodists, the original Catholic Church and many other de...nom...i...na...tions." He said the word very slowly.

"Oh, well, we're Baptists."

"There you go, Grant. Christians have more denominations than Muslims, although there are a few, such as the biggest, *Sunni*, next the *Shi'a*, and the *Sufi* and *Sikh*, a blend of Islam and Hinduism."

"What I can't get, Sergeant, is that they're all Muslims. Why do they fight each other so?"

Burns sighed. "Look, Grant, the Christian faith has much blood on its hands, most notably the bloodbath between the Protestants and Catholics in Europe. The Catholic Church has a dismal record of persecuting, even executing Jews and others during the inquisitions. Didn't you pay attention in history class?"

"Naw." He lowered the *Stars and Stripes* he'd been reading. "I barely made it through eleventh grade and had to get my G.E.D. I couldn't pass the high school exit exam they started in California. We didn't have that in Alabama."

Burns shifted in his seat. "Well, you'll just have to take a course in religion when you get home. You should at least go to a community college and get a two-year degree, in nothing but general studies that you can build upon later if you decide. But that is what I am paid for. So don't think you're going to get it from me for free."

"Thanks, Sergeant. You're a real pal."

Burns placed his book, a biography on Guru Nanak, the founder of the Sikh religion, on the table next to the sofa he sat on. He withdrew a fresh cigar from his breast pocket. His daughter Sara, back in New Orleans, sent him a fresh supply every month.

He walked out of the common room and made his way over to the smoking area. He saw the usual suspects gathered there getting their nicotine fixes including Major McCollum, who was in charge of security. He also saw Colonel Petersen, who was in charge of supply logistics, getting his fix to calm his nerves because an army couldn't do anything without bullets and bread.

Before he could light his cigar, however, Lieutenant Fischer approached, Major Cunningham at her side.

"Sergeant Burns," said Fischer. "This is Major Cunningham. He needs to speak with you."

Burns came to attention, then shook the major's hand. "Major," he said.

Chapter Eight

Two Iraqi men stopped in front of office 27b. "This is the one," said the young man. He scanned the corridor while the other man unlocked the door with a key on a large ring.

The younger man was the cafeteria worker who had tailed Cunningham to his office earlier that day. The older man, dressed in an Iraqi uniform, opened the door. The cafeteria worker followed him in and closed the door behind them.

The uniformed man turned on the light and scanned Cunningham's office. It had a small wooden desk, a chair near the door, another in front of the desk and a filing cabinet against the wall. He moved toward the desk, turned on a small desk lamp, and searched through papers. The cafeteria worker watched over him.

The uniformed man noticed handwritten notes on a pad.

"What do you see?" asked the cafeteria worker.

The uniformed man flipped a page and read more notes. "Two names, a Professor al-Hakim of Islamic studies in Cambridge, England, and a Sergeant Burns with the U.S. Army. The word necklace is circled many times and the name A'isha is written here." He glanced up at the young man.

"Burns is the name I heard the major say in the cafeteria. Something about him being a professor of Christianity and Islam and an important mission he was to do for them."

"I think this confirms what it is we are looking for," said the uniformed man. He straightened Cunningham's notepad, pulled a scrap of paper out of his pocket, and wrote down the names. He fumbled with keys on his key ring, and finding one, he unlocked the filing cabinet and pulled open the top drawer. He fingered through several files until he came upon the file on Sergeant Burns that Cunningham had read that day. He used a small camera and photographed the contents of each page. The file also contained information on Burns' daughter.

He replaced the file and found another one on Professor al-Hakim of the University of Cambridge. As he photographed this file, he skimmed the dossier because he was curious of this Iraqi. He learned al-Hakim was a visiting professor of Middle Eastern and Islamic studies from The University of Cairo. An Islamic scholar, an *alim*, he was an Iraqi *Shiite* by birth. He hadn't been back to Iraq since before the commencement of Operation Iraqi Freedom in March 2003. He had been fortunate to get his family out because many in the intellectual community were later murdered. He had been teaching at The University of Cairo for two years. Before his assignment in Cairo, he had taught at Baghdad University.

Fingering though the pages, the uniformed man continued to learn al-Hakim and his wife had three children, now fully grown. Johara, his wife, had stayed in Cairo at the university hospital as a medical technician. Together they had one son in Jordan working as a doctor in the King Hussein Hospital and two daughters in Cairo, one who taught at the university in microbiology and another daughter who had married a businessman and was now raising a family.

The last section the uniformed man photographed and skimmed centered on al-Hakim's area of expertise, the beginnings of Islam, particularly the *Sunni* and *Shiite* split after the death of Muhammad in 632 AD.

He replaced the file on al-Hakim and found another one on Jabber Hassef. He took pictures of that file too. It outlined a purported necklace belonging to A'isha rumored to be in Hassef's possession. He replaced the file and closed the cabinet, locking it. "You have done well for your *Shiite* brothers. Al-Salah will continue to reward your family."

He made sure he put back everything in its place and that nothing was out of order. They turned off the light, opened the door and went out. After scanning the hallway, they closed the door and walked off.

The Lost *Hadīth*

Burns sat with Cunningham at a table in the smoking area. Cunningham reached in and pulled from his briefcase the necklace with the attached dangling pendant, handing it to Burns.

Burns ran the beads through his fingers and examined the pendant. He read the inscriptions, which he could easily decipher, and, flipping it over, studied the depictions. His face tightened as he flipped it over again to re-read the inscriptions. He turned it over yet again and analyzed the depictions once more.

"What do you think, Professor? Can you understand it?"

He glanced over at Cunningham. "Where did you get this?" He looked back down at the necklace and pendant and studied them some more.

"An Iraqi *Sunni* had it. Apparently it had been passed down to him for safekeeping a long time ago."

"I've heard rumors of this, didn't think it was true. Even if I had thought it was true, I never believed this could ever be found." He considered this a moment while shaking his head. "I know what it says," he said continuing, "but it's a riddle of some sort."

Cunningham waited for him to digest all of this. "Do you think you can figure it out?"

"It would have to be studied and debated by experts." He slid the necklace back and forth through his fingers. "Scholars accept the story of the necklace, but can this truly be the one? I mean, in my hands?" He looked down at the necklace cradled in the palm of his hand. "Sure, within religious and academic circles, particularly Islamic ones, most believed that if it were true and still out there, it had been lost forever, like the Arc of the Covenant, or the Holy Grail."

"Do you think there's a chance this pendant can lead to these so-called lost writings?"

"I don't know, Major. It could be a wild goose chase. *Shiites* believe *Sunnis* made this all up to hold sway over them."

"This *hadīth*? I understand it is a journal?"

"Sayings, observations. Scholars view them as the written record of

Muhammad's life. It records Muhammad's so-called *Sunnah*, a trodden path. The *ḥadīth,* or in Arabic plural, *aḥādīth,* are believed to be a complete and final record by many *ulema,* Islamic scholars, of his journey and teachings. These *aḥādīth,* similar to the New Testament of the Christian Bible, where some gospels were included and some excluded by clergy, were included and others excluded because of the split and subsequent rift between the warring factions after Muhammad's death. Some could be verified and some could not. Others were excluded because of what they contained, such as controversial or contradictory interpretations."

"You're comparing this exclusion to the Gospels of Saint Thomas, Mary Magdalene and others?"

"Right. Powerful men, when the Catholic Church was still being formed, decided which gospels to include and which to exclude. There were communities that adhered to and followed one particular Gospel, say Thomas, but it depended on the power of one community over another when the faith began to merge into the Universal, or Catholic Church, that decided which gospels to include in the official book and which ones to discard. Many point to the Councils of Constantinople, under Constantine, as deciding, or compiling the Gospels and other letters of the New Testament. Scholars still dispute these councils and their outcomes. Scholars also still dispute who wrote the Gospels because they weren't written until many years, decades, after Christ's death and the deaths of his apostles.

"With Islam," Burns continued, "it was Muhammad's *sahabah,* his companions, such as his wife A'isha and her father, Abu Bakr, who became the first *caliph* in Islam upon Muhammad's death, who compiled the central collections of *aḥādīth.* Bakr was one of Muhammad's closet companions who, along with A'isha, helped him interpret his dreams. In addition, Muslims believe the *Qur'an* was transmitted via the Archangel Gabriel to Muhammad by way of visions and dreams, from God over the course of twenty years, beginning around Muhammad's fortieth year. However, similar to the Christian *Bible,* and both the *Torah* and the Jewish *Talmud* before it, the *Qur'an* was told orally. It was told and memorized like the oral tradition of the day and repeated by Muhammad's followers who then had it written down. Many orthodox Muslims today memorize and recite it as part of their schooling, in the vein of Muhammad's original followers. It was then finally compiled into one book by Usman ibn 'Affān, the third *caliph,* after Muhammad's death.

"Similar to the *Qur'an* and these *aḥādīth*," Burns went on, resembling a professor giving a lecture, "the Jewish books and the New Testament weren't written down by those who originally told the stories. They were written much later. With the New Testament, it wasn't until the first generation of Jesus' followers began dying off that the Gospels were finally written down."

"The Gospels," Burns said, running the necklace through his fingers again, "both the included and excluded ones, in the vein of these *aḥādīth*, were also compiled in a similar way. Muhammad's scribes and confidants, such as A'isha, wrote down his stories and sayings. There are differing interpretations of events, sayings and actions of Muhammad, similar to Christ, as written in the New Testament. Even though the adherent to each faith proclaims their book in particular and their faith in general, is the exact word of God, these texts were written by men. Men are fallible, men are selective, and men are motivational relative to their cause, their point of view. Did God tell Constantine which Gospels to include and which to exclude? Did Allah tell Bakr which *ḥadīth* to include and which to discard?" He studied the markings on the pendant again.

"Do you think this could really be the lost necklace of A'isha, professor?"

"It's possible. Or an elaborate hoax."

"What exactly is the necklace of A'isha?"

"A'isha claimed she had left camp early one morning for personal hygiene and had lost her necklace. She then spent some time searching for it, but when she returned to the camp, the camp had departed without her. She was accused by some of Muhammad's closest confidants of having an affair with the man who had rescued her. Muhammad later had a vision from God exonerating her, although *Shiite* Muslims dispute this, I think in great deal to the fact she had later raised an army and had battled Ali, the fourth *Caliph*. Alī ibn Abī Ṭālib, or simply Ali, was Muhammad's cousin and son-in-law."

"Really?" Cunningham said, raising his eyebrow.

"It's a long story. Anyway, for *Sunni* Muslims, A'isha is very revered and is believed responsible for at least one fourth of the collections of *aḥādīth*."

"No kidding?" said Cunningham. "This could all make sense. This lost *ḥadīth*, her necklace, this pendant, her being responsible for much of these *aḥādīth*."

"She was integral in supporting Muhammad and getting him to accept his prophecy as well as interpreting the revelations he received, particularly after the death of his first wife, Khadijah. A'isha was believed to be his favorite wife."

Burns handed the necklace back to Cunningham and reached for the cigar in his pocket that he had wanted to light earlier. "Do you mind if we take a walk and I light up?"

"No, not at all," Cunningham said.

Burns lit his cigar and they walked slowly around the base, Cunningham carrying his briefcase and holding the necklace. It was a signature Middle Eastern night with the crescent moon hanging brightly above them in the cloudless sky. Stars twinkled by the millions. "I think you know," Burns said, "you have a potentially explosive and controversial artifact there. If its authenticity can be confirmed, this is serious business. I'm not sure where this could lead."

Cunningham stopped abruptly. "That's why we want you to investigate, confirm its authenticity, and if you can decipher the riddle, find these lost writings. You would be on special assignment for us."

Burns glanced over at him and said, "Who are we?" He drew in a deep puff and blew out thick, grey smoke.

"Well, I'm not at liberty to say exactly who the we are, but the we are high on the chain."

"I see."

"You would report to me, and only me. We want to keep those with the need-to-know to a minimum. My office is in the Green Zone, but I will get to you specific instructions on how to contact me. You must never report there."

"This is all real cloak and dagger?" Burns tapped his cigar, knocking some ash onto the ground.

Cunningham chuckled. "You could say."

Burns contemplated this adventure. It all seemed very enticing. He could be a part of an important discovery, for the sake of historical reference. What this could do for his career, his place in history, might be significant. He gazed up at the stars twinkling in the sky and saw that attractive woman strolling arm-in-arm with him on the bank of the River Seine. He saw his young daughter running over to hug him while he sat at his desk working on papers back home in California. He considered he might be abandoning his young soldiers. "I don't know," Burns said. "I, ah, think you've got the wrong guy."

"I understand your apprehension, Professor."

Burns squinted at Cunningham and took another drag on his cigar.

"Think about how important this could be," Cunningham said, staring at Burns. "You're perfectly situated here. You know this subject. You'll have the full support and resources of the U.S. government behind you. This could be a most substantial discovery."

Burns flicked some more ash at his feet and ground it into the sand with the tip of his boot. "Well, I would need expert assistance to help decipher this pendant and confirm its authenticity. My colleague, Doctor Ahmed al-Hakim in Cairo, actually he's a visiting professor at the University of Cambridge, is the preeminent authority on these matters."

"Yes. We have already learned this and know of your collegiate relationship."

Burns cracked a smile and puffed on his cigar. He clearly understood who the we might be with that disclosure. That probably meant Cunningham, although a major in the U.S. Army, doubled for the CIA, probably with the Special Activities Division, a division that coordinated Black Operations and other covert operations. *Government liaison office? Indeed*, thought Burns.

"I'll have your orders drawn up. You'll have a Canadian passport, so as not to complicate matters."

"Of course." Burns wondered what the hell Cunningham or the we were getting him into. However, with the lure of ancient secrets, and his potential place in history, he couldn't resist. "It's not so much a favor, is it?"

"We really need your expertise on this, Professor."

Burns sighed. "I see."

Cunningham jiggled the necklace in the palm of his hand and handed it to Burns.

Burns calculated the necklace and pendant and gazed up at the crescent moon again, deliberating.

"What is it, Professor?"

"Well, my platoon and their safety without me."

"I understand. I read a report on you and your National Guard tenure. You have trained your men well over the years. Your men are capable soldiers. They're in good hands. They'll make it without you."

Burns blew out cigar smoke after taking a drag. "Yes, well, I guess we're all expendable." He flicked some more ash onto the ground. "No, you're right. They should be fine." He shifted and continued walking. "What do the we plan on doing with this *ḥadīth*, assuming it exists and I can find it?" He waited for Cunningham to answer, but Cunningham only walked beside him in silence.

Burns nodded. "You haven't yet figured that out yet."

"Well, to be honest, Professor, we'll assess that concern at that time."

"I see."

Early the next morning, the young cafeteria worker skulked through the Baghdad streets. He made his way over to a Baghdad bazaar that had seen an increase in business because of the American surge. He stood there on the street scanning the patrons who scurried around. He tried to be watchful so no undue attention would befall him. He hovered on the side of the street near a vegetable cart.

He saw the tall man approaching in the opposite direction. Abdullah Nasir Yassim was dressed in typical Iraqi dress, a large white *Galabia*, skullcap, and wore his beard long, in the vein of al-Salah. In his middle forties, he had a long face and carried himself like a man of importance. He reminded many who crossed his path of *al-Qaeda* leader and master terrorist Osama bin Laden.

The cafeteria worker cowered next to the vegetable cart as Yassim approached. "You have the information, my brother?" Yassim said.

"Yes." His hand shaking, he passed Yassim a paper with writing. He scanned the streets as Yassim examined the paper, folded it and tucked it inside his *Galabia*. Yassim handed him a wad of Iraqi dinar. "You have done well, Mustafa. The Brotherhood will continue to reward your efforts. Do not be careless and allow your *Shiite* brothers to suspect you are working for us. Contact me only if you have more information."

Mustafa fingered through the bills, pocketed them, and scampered down the street. Yassim strolled off in the opposite direction.

Major Cunningham entered his office early this morning. He placed his briefcase in the chair opposite his desk. He sat down and noticed his notepad slightly askew. He cocked his head as a young female lieutenant entered his office carrying a file folder.

"Here's the file on Yassim you requested, Major." She handed it to him.

"Thank you, Lieutenant."

She headed back towards the door.

"Lieutenant?"

"Yes, sir?"

"Anyone been in here this morning?"

"No, sir. Anything wrong?"

"Not sure. Thank you."

She nodded and departed. Cunningham was an orderly man. Not a notebook, not a pen or pencil, nothing was out of order on his desk or in his office. He straightened his notepad and opened the file on Yassim. As with al-Salah, he knew Yassim also wished to acquire the necklace and had been warring with al-Salah for some time. Therefore, he wanted to study-up on Yassim.

He read how Abdullah Nasir Yassim grew up in an upper middle class Egyptian family. His father was a well-respected merchant who had made a fortune in the tourist trade. The company made and sold trinkets and other souvenirs for tourists, mostly westerners. Young Yassim had been groomed by his father to take over the business someday, but the young Yassim became bored, having been spoiled as a child. His father had sent him to Cairo University, making him major in business studies. Yassim graduated, but tired of his father and the westerners who paraded through his country to gape at their ancient pagan symbols. He found the western tourists rude and faithless.

A couple years out of college, and drudging along in his father's company, Yassim met the leader of, then joined, the Brotherhood of Bakr. He completely severed his ties from his father and the family business at the urgings of Brotherhood members, but not before stealing much of his father's vast fortune. He promptly gave all the money to the Brotherhood.

Cunningham turned the page and took a gulp of water from a bottle on his desk. He read how Brotherhood of Bakr leader Ammar Kamil Ashur had readied the young Yassim to take over for him upon his death. That happened in 2003. Yassim took over and led the Brotherhood, taking it in a more radical direction, challenging the legitimacy and rule of Egyptian President Hosni Mubarak. Mubarak had been accused by the Brotherhood as being too supportive of western influence.

The main purpose of the Brotherhood's founding nearly a century earlier had been to safeguard the legitimacy of the *Sunni* doctrine and the teachings of Abu Bakr. Additionally, *Sunnis* in general and the Brotherhood in particular, greatly revered A'isha, as she was not only Muhammad's beloved wife, but also Bakr's daughter.

However, over the last fifty years the Brotherhood had taken a more active role in influencing political events, most notably the Palestinian/Israeli conflict. The Brotherhood sought to establish in Egypt an Islamic *caliphate*, a theocratic state based on traditional governance, or *Sharia* law, similar to what the Taliban had done in Afghanistan.

Through backchannels, the black market, and the underworld, Yassim, during his tenure, funneled resources to terrorist groups throughout the Middle East. These groups attacked Iraqis, Americans, Jordanians, British interests and Israelis.

Another aim for the Brotherhood was challenging the emerging influence of *Shiites* throughout the world, most notably in Iraq and Iran.

The file concluded with an analysis of how Yassim figured that if he could get the necklace, and what it was rumored to lead to, a lost *ḥadīth*, then he could hold sway over his misguided *Shiite* brothers. He had to get hold of this *ḥadīth* before his sworn enemy and rival Hasan Ali al-Salah obtained and destroyed the necklace and its secrets.

Cunningham finally learned how Yassim tried to kill al-Salah several times. He finished reading the file, slipped it into his filing cabinet and locked it. He then called his wife in New York.

Chapter Nine

Dr. Ahmed al-Hakim hurried along Silver Street in Cambridge, England. The warm July day provided the perfect excuse for many students at the university to skip their summer course of study and lounge around on the riverbank. Tourists meandered as well admiring the campus. Al-Hakim smiled at the young scholars and tourists. He knew all too well that it rained much in England so you had to take advantage of this blessing when you had the chance.

He crossed the River Cam. Several men and women punted along in their flat-bottom, square-cut boats. He glanced at his watch. He would have just enough time to go back to his flat and get the exams he had graded for his students for his afternoon class. He had forgotten to bring them earlier.

At fifty-three years of age, he had a narrow Arabic face, a closely cropped salt and pepper beard, olive brown skin, and dark brown eyes. He bordered a bus on Queen's Road and Sidgwick Avenue and made it back to his flat in West Cambridge a few minutes later.

He rushed up the stairs to the second floor. At his age, he was in great shape, but slowed when he discovered his door ajar. *Odd*, he thought. He knew his students referred to him as the perennial absent-minded professor, but he always pulled his door closed because it self-locked.

He swung open the door to his flat and discovered it had been ransacked. Everything was topsy-turvy. His books, papers, and clothes from his armoire were strewn about. "Hoodlums," he whispered. He figured it had been a random burglary because he had nothing of any value. He found the exams scattered on the floor amongst the rest of his scholarly papers. He gathered the exams and placed them in his briefcase, pulled the door closed behind him, wiggling the handle to ensure it had indeed locked. He shrugged it off and trotted down the stairs.

He hopped on the bus a minute later, and it sped down Barton Road towards the university. He didn't notice the two chaps watching him from inside a white Lexus SUV that pulled out and followed the bus.

Fatima sat in the passenger's seat of a car that drove into the departure terminal at the Los Angeles International Airport.

The car pulled up and stopped at the curb in front of the Saudi Airlines gate at the Tom Bradley International terminal. She waited, staring out the windshield for the longest time, a younger Burns tapping his fingers on the steering wheel beside her. "I really wish you would come," she finally said.

He sighed and said, "We've been over this."

Silence.

"You know how important this is for my career," he said, looking over at her.

More silence.

"She'll understand, if you don't go," he said.

"I have to see her one more time." She looked over at him, pursed her lips and sighed. "I really owe her for all we have."

"I know, but, this is just not a good time, with the conference."

A car behind them tooted its horn. "I've got to go," he said. She leaned over, gave him a quick parting kiss and crawled out of the car. Dressed in a tight-fitting shirt and jeans, she grabbed her handbag, draped it over her shoulder, opened the rear door, and pulled out a small suitcase.

"Call me when you get there," Burns said. "Love you."

She nodded at him, closed the car door and watched him drive away.

"Sergeant Burns?" an Air force lieutenant said. "Sergeant Burns?"

Staring at the floor daydreaming, Burns was dressed in civilian cargo pants and a golf shirt. Waiting for his flight at Baghdad International Airport, his long face looked up at her.

"Your flight is now boarding." She handed him his papers.

"Oh. Yes. Thank you, Lieutenant." He grabbed his leather satchel and military duffle bag and walked across the tarmac. Baghdad International Airport, formally Saddam International Airport, was beginning its transition back into civilian hands after United States Military control.

Cunningham intercepted him at the foot of the stairs to the C17 Globemaster transport plane. He handed Burns a large manila envelope. "This contains everything you need," Cunningham said. "Good luck."

"Thanks, Major." He shook his hand and climbed the steps to the aircraft.

On board Burns settled in. The interior of the aircraft had red mesh seating. Soldiers sat there lined up and down the length of the plane, not from side to side of the aircraft as in a civilian flight. He sat strapped in near the front section. A young battle-weary captain sat on one side and a sleepy lieutenant on the other. The captain glanced over at him when he opened the envelope and pulled out the contents. Burns shot him a smile, not as in happy to see you, but as in mind your own business. The captain turned away and opened the latest James Patterson novel.

Burns found his Canadian passport; he was now a Canadian. His picture was his military one glued onto the fake passport. He unclipped a credit card from a piece of paper with a twenty thousand dollar credit limit and a note rubber-banded to it. The credit card was from the Royal British Bank of England. The note indicated the personal identification number as his date of birth.

He also found a bank statement and a debit card from The Royal Saudi Bank. The account was in his name and showed a twenty thousand dollar balance. This bank had branches scattered all over the Middle East and Europe. The note attached to it from Cunningham read:

> *You may need cash for enticement. As you can see, the PIN on this account is Independence Day, 07041776.*

How they did all this in such short order, he had no idea. He found a cell phone with international service and instructions on how to contact Cunningham. At the bottom of the paper, Cunningham had written:

> *Only text with this phone, Sergeant. I'd like to say this will self-destruct in five minutes, but we're not that sophisticated. You should, however, flush the bank statement and my notes down the toilet after completing your reading. Yes, it's clandestine, Professor. You need to be cautious. Our intelligence confirms several Islamic groups are aware of the necklace's discovery and actively pursuing it.*

Now he tells me this? he said to himself. *What's he getting him into, or better still, what's the we getting him into?*

He pocketed his passport in his cargo pants pocket and put the credit and debit cards in his wallet. He texted a message to Sara:

> *Sara. I'm not on base. On special assignment. Text me at this number: 0330 44 330803145.*

The plane taxied and lifted off into the afternoon sun. He unbuckled his harness and headed to the restroom where he did indeed tear up the papers into small pieces and flush them down the toilet. He returned to his seat and finished reading the book on Guru Nanak while en route to Germany.

Chapter Ten

The Great Mosque of Ali in Baghdad overflowed with worshipers in the late afternoon sun. Men outside who hadn't gained access squatted on the ground near the entrance running their prayer beads through their fingers. Old men, young men, sick men, rich men, poor men, all sat listening to their imam's voice blaring out to them on speakers that had been placed outside the walls.

The mosque was enormous, built in traditional Iraqi architecture centuries ago. Two minarets rose to the heavens on either side of the large golden Dome. The ubiquitous Arabic half moon and star at the top stood out. The outer front of the building entrance, painted distinctively beige, had tiled mosaics pasted on it. The sun bathed the entire building in an enormous glow, as if Allah himself shined his approval down upon his followers.

Inside, a thousand followers sat on the floor in nearly perfect rows listing to Grand Ayatollah Ali Mohammad Kasem. Kasem was a man in his later years, perhaps seventy years old or so because birth records were not always kept or weren't as accurate in much of the region. He had a full white beard and was dressed in typical imam dress, a black robe and *Amamah*.

The inside of the mosque was as spectacular as the exterior. Mosaics adorned the walls depicting scenes of Ali in battle against Muhammad's enemies, polytheists, other apostates and depictions of the *Ridda* wars, also known as the Wars of Apostasy.

There were no women to be seen anywhere at this time. This day and hour was only for men to listen to the imam deliver a sermon on the infidels who continued to occupy their sacred ground. In addition, Kasem lectured on and on about how they must not kill their brothers and to follow Allah's law of compassion. The supporters would from time to time, at the right moment, pause, as allowed by Kasem, raise their voices in agreement, and say, *"alhamdulillah," praise be to Allah.*

Sitting behind Kasem and to his right side near other bearded, robed men, Hasan Ali al-Salah nodded his head in agreement.

Ayatollah Kasem finished his address, and the men there chanted his name. He raised his right arm, palm down, and slowly waved it over the crowd, as if to bless them. He sat down in a chair behind the lectern.

The crowd then chanted "al-Salah" repeatedly until he finally stood up behind the lectern. He too raised his right arm and waved it over the crowd. The mosque simmered down.

Kasem glanced at another cleric who sat near him. The cleric looked back at Kasem and raised his left eyebrow. The last time al-Salah had spoken, Kasem remembered, he had rallied against his *Sunni* brothers and the Americans whom he claimed were out to destroy their holy sites. The result had been an increase in executions of *Sunni* officials, doctors, and bombings in *Sunni* neighborhoods killing thousands of civilians, including many women and children. It took three months until the activity had decreased to the levels that had been occurring before his fiery speech.

"My brothers," al-Salah began. "In the name of Allah, the infinitely compassionate and merciful. Praise be to Allah, Lord of all the worlds. The compassionate, the merciful. Ruler on the day of reckoning. You alone do we worship, and You alone do we ask for help. Guide us on the straight path, the path of those who have received your grace. Not the path of those who have brought down wrath, nor of those who wander astray. Amen."

During this *Salat*, the Islamic prayer, the entire gathering went prostrate, with their forehead, nose, palms of both hands, knees, and toes all touching the floor. They faced the *Qiblah*, the direction one should face when praying, towards the *Ka'aba* in *Mecca*.

Al-Salah continued, "O Allah, bless our Muhammad and the people of Muhammad, as you have blessed Abraham and the people of Abraham. Surely, you are the Praiseworthy, the Glorious. O Allah, be gracious unto Muhammad and the people of Muhammad, as you were gracious unto Abraham and the people of Abraham. Surely you are the Praiseworthy, the

Glorious."

The entire gathering again performed *Salat* facing the *Qiblah*.

After the prayer, al-Salah paused and scanned the large ornate grand colonnade and the opulent columns that supported the decorative ceiling. The great room grew silent as a quiet desert night. "My brothers," al-Salah started again, the entire mosque in the palm of his hand. His face tightened. "We face a grave danger. A blasphemous enemy is seeking to destroy us, our way of life." He clenched his fist and raised it into the air.

A rumbling murmur spread throughout the vast chamber.

"It has come to my attention that there are forces out to desecrate our holy lands. We must be vigilant! We must take notice! The infidels are looking to dig up the graves of our holy ones."

"No!" dozens of followers shouted.

"I have received news that the Americans, and yes, I must say, some of our *Sunni* brothers have been led astray and are looking to destroy *Shi'a* Islam in concert with the Americans."

"No!" the thousands shouted again.

"Death to the infidels!" a young, scrawny, bearded man bellowed.

Kasem fidgeted in his chair. He tried to remain calm. He needed to get al-Salah off the stage and diffuse the situation before another bloodletting began.

Al-Salah raised his arms up and down several times, palms down. "Now, now, my brothers. We must not act in haste, but we must be alert. We must return to our homes, and spread the word throughout Iraq for all Muslims to be on guard. Keep on guard for anyone scouring near mosques, tombs, holy sites, especially Americans."

Kasem had met with the Americans a few weeks ago to broker a peace plan. Most Iraqi's wanted the Americans gone, but Kasem was wise enough to know they wouldn't leave before Iraq was at least more stable. With more violence, Kasim figured, either against the Americans, or amongst the Iraqis themselves, the Iraqi police, backed up by the American military, would swoop in and clamp down again causing even more bloodshed in the process of bringing peace.

As the crowd chanted, raising its arms and fists up and down, an explosion reverberated outside the mosque. Al-Salah, jolted backwards, managed to hold onto the lectern. Many parishioners panicked and stampeded towards the exits. Armed, masked men, gripping AK-47s in the ready position, rushed al-Salah and whisked him off the stage and through the back of the mosque. They stuffed him into his SUV and sped way.

Kasem and the other clerics ran out the back also, but they stayed in the area to help with the wounded and to calm the angry crowd.

A car bomb had exploded on the street in front of the mosque. A dozen innocent Iraqis passing by had been killed, many more wounded. The bombers turned out to be al-Qaeda in Iraq. They had learned about the gathering and wanted to stir things up.

Stir things up they did. Many of the mosque attendees spread a rumor the Americans had bombed the meeting. "Death to America!" many shouted. "Death to the infidels." They jumped up and down in the streets, their fists in the air, some firing their weapons at the clouds.

Chapter Eleven

After staying late into the night at the bedside of her sick and dying sister, Fatima hired a taxi to take her back to her hotel in the early-morning hours. She waited for the elevator and went up to her room.

She entered the room, closed the door and removed her *hijāb* and veil. As she did, a man stood up from the sofa.

Startled, Fatima dropped her room key and handbag. The man moved towards her, studying her closely. She flipped the light switch and the lights came on. "Jamal?" she said, freezing in her footsteps.

He edged closer to her. "It is you!" He squinted at her, and his face tightened into a rage.

"Yes. What do you want?"

"You dishonored Father. You disobeyed the will of Allah." He unsheathed a *jambiya*, a short curved blade he had in his belt. "You must die for your sins." Jamal was a small and disheveled man, his face greasy and hair dirty. He lunged for her, but she blocked his attack. As tall as he, she struggled with him but managed to hold his wrist, the one holding the dagger. He pushed her up against the wall with the weight of his body.

She gained the upper hand and forced the dagger back towards him. It sliced across his right cheek from his ear to his chin. He screamed in agony, but held onto the dagger.

She took advantage of his pain and disorientation and again turned the knife on him, this time stabbing him in his left eye.

He wailed, dropped the *jambiya* and put his hands up to his left eye.

She tried to make it back to the door, but he was on her swiftly. Bleeding from his wounded eye, he tackled her.

She kicked at him several times, striking him in the face and the chest. She sprung to her feet and tried to open the door, but he jumped up and pulled her back.

He grabbed her arm with his right hand, spun her around and threw her to the floor again. He kicked her in the chest, sucking the air out of her lungs.

He held his left hand over his bleeding left eye, picked the *jambiya* up off the floor with his right hand, and rushed her as she struggled to catch her breath.

Burns snapped out of his daydream as his flight landed at the massive U.S. airbase at Ramstein, Germany in the middle of the night.

He caught an early train to Frankfurt and booked a civilian flight to Heathrow. Before he bordered his London flight, he bought a civilian backpack and discarded the military duffle bag. He sorted through his items and downsized so he didn't have as much to carry. *Hell*, he thought, *he had twenty thousand dollars and a credit card that had another twenty thousand dollar limit, so he could afford to buy new clothes every day. This was some operation*, he considered. *The U.S. government wanted all this for what?* They must want to find this *ḥadīth* and keep it out of the hands of fanatics. He had always thought the necklace was lost forever, and certainly, this excluded *ḥadīth* as well, but the rumors had persisted inside scholarly circles for centuries. Well, he'd worry about the government's motives later. The thrill of discovery, and something that could have a profound impact on his place in history, drove him forward in this quest.

Upon landing at Heathrow, he caught a train out to Cambridge. Once the train had passed through the outskirts of London, the green countryside became a refreshing break from the dusty streets of Baghdad. He watched sheep, cows and a host of other farm animals grazing from the window of his train. He didn't bother reading or doing anything else but enjoyed watching the ancient, English landscape roll by.

In Cambridge, he went straight to the offices of the Centre of Middle Eastern and Islamic Studies on Sedgwick Avenue. He approached a young clerk behind the counter and found the whereabouts of Professor al-Hakim. He had been to Cambridge University before, but he still grabbed a campus map and had the clerk highlight his route to the lecture hall where al-Hakim was finishing a lecture.

On his trek to the hall, he admired the architectural beauty and character of this eight hundred year-old campus. He waited outside the door until the lecture concluded five minutes later.

As the students filed past him, he entered and approached al-Hakim who stood talking to students near the front of the hall. Al-Hakim peered over at him, his face lighting up with a big smile. "Patrick," he said. "Please excuse me," he said to the students. "A friend from far away has come to call. We can talk about your exams and concerns at another time." The students sauntered off. He rushed over to Burns and enthusiastically shook his hand.

"It's good to see you too, Ahmed," Burns said.

"What a pleasure it is," al-Hakim said. Although al-Hakim spoke clear English, albeit with a thick accent, he did not contract his English words. "What brings you to Cambridge?"

"I've come for your help. Shall we sit?" Burns motioned to a seat nearby.

"My office is down the hall. We can go there."

He followed al-Hakim to his office. The office was small and had one window looking out onto a quad with bright green grass and fresh flowers. Al-Hakim picked some books up off the chair opposite his cluttered desk. "Please, sit, my friend." His office was full of books, piles of student papers to grade, and a half-eaten sandwich on his desk that he picked up and threw into the trashcan. As he sat, he said, "I'm still very sorry for your loss, Patrick."

"Thank you, Ahmed." He shifted in the chair.

Al-Hakim's face grew long and he fidgeted in his chair too. "And Jamal was never held accountable?"

Burns shook his head, pursing his lips.

"I am so ashamed sometimes by our antiquated customs." He looked at Burns and frowned. "Well, would you like some water, Patrick?" He bolted from his chair to open his refrigerator.

"Yes, thank you, Ahmed."

"How is little Sara?" Al-Hakim handed him a bottle of water and sat back down.

"Not so little. She's a graduate student at Tulane University. She actually completed her undergraduate work in two and a half years."

"Wonderful. She is just like her mother then."

"Yeah, looks just like her too." He sipped some water. "Well, I need you to take a look at something I'm working on, Ahmed." He pulled the necklace off from around his neck and handed it to him.

Al-Hakim took the necklace and studied the beads. He next examined the side of the pendant with the writings. He turned it over to the other side and studied the engravings. He turned it back again, his mouth dropping open.

"You are thinking what I am thinking?"

"Where did you find this?"

"In Iraq. It had apparently been in the possession of a prominent *Sunni* executive who dealt heavily in the black market. I was told he had it for many years and had been blackmailing both *Sunni* and *Shi'a* clergy."

Al-Hakim continued studying the pendant. "Can this be? I have always believed it would never be found."

"I had the same reaction."

He looked up at him. "Is it possible that this is it?"

Burns nodded. "Possible."

Al-Hakim considered the necklace again, examining the beads. He ran them through his fingers then inspected the pendant more closely. "And these markings?" He touched his index finger on them. "Could they be clues that lead to the lost and missing collection of the *ahādīth*? The chapters A'isha had written?"

"The ones rumored to have been excluded by her father in the official collection," Burns said.

"Oh my. If this is true, this is significant. This is historical. Do you know what this could mean? To Islam?" His face tightened.

"Yes," Burns said. "That's what I'm afraid of."

Al-Hakim thought a moment. "Or not. Maybe affirmation."

Burns was glad for his optimism, but he knew if it had been reaffirming, then it would have been included in the official collections of *ahādīth*.

"Well, anyway," al-Hakim said, probably not believing what he himself had just said, "we are historians, Patrick. We only seek the truth no matter where this takes us. We must follow our code." Once more he scrutinized the writings and the symbols on the pendant. "This is fascinating," he said, running his fingers over the markings again.

"The writings are riddles and the etchings additional clues as to where the lost *ḥadīth* might be."

"Yes," al-Hakim said, again studying the side of the pendant that had the writings. "I am still in disbelief that this could have belonged to A'isha, and it is right here in my hands, but it says:

عائشة ام المؤمنين

"*A'isha, Umm al-mu'minin.* Mother of the Believers," Burns said, translating. "I think we need to first establish the necklace and pendant's origin, age, and be certain they are genuine."

"Yes. I agree." Al-Hakim sighed. "This necklace, the beads are clearly ancient Yemenite. Partly black and partly white. They match the description as recorded in official records." He shook his head slowly. "I still do not believe what I am possibly holding in my hands." He looked up at Burns. "The necklace of A'isha, wife of the Prophet Muhammad."

"A'isha and the necklace," Burns said, nodding. "It's like finding the Holy Grail."

"Or the Dead Sea Scrolls."

"Yes, Ahmed, but as we agree, this is potentially dangerous. We must proceed cautiously and tell no one of this, yet."

Al-Hakim nodded. "Yes, of course. I have a colleague here whose specialty is Arabic and Mesopotamian archaeology. He is quite good. I trust him completely. Let us go to him now." Burns followed him out of the office and into the quad between the two ancient buildings, an area once traversed by King Henry VIII.

Chapter Twelve

The white SUV that had followed al-Hakim earlier sat parked on Pembroke Street. The two young men inside were of Middle Eastern descent. The passenger spotted Burns walking with al-Hakim.

Both men, in their middle twenties, were dressed in Western attire, slacks, golf shirts and tennis shoes. They were close shaven and had short hair. The passenger considered the two photographs he held of Burns and al-Hakim. He elbowed the driver awake and signaled towards the two men. "It is them," the passenger said.

"Okay," said the driver. "Wait until they turn on Saint Andrew's Street." The driver started the vehicle and followed at a slow pace down the street, keeping a safe distance.

Burns and al-Hakim turned left onto Saint Andrew's Street. Al-Hakim dangled the pendant on the necklace in his hand, looking at it occasionally.

The SUV pulled up and stopped short of the intersection, blocking traffic. Both men jumped out and headed for the professors.

"Hey!" a motorist yelled out his driver's window. "You can't park there." He honked his horn several times.

Burns caught the commotion out of the corner of his eye and saw two men charging in his direction. "Watch it, Ahmed!" he shouted.

The passenger man pulled out a two-inch knife. Burns swung his backpack at him, knocking the knife out of his hand and promptly sucker-punched him in the face. The man fell to the ground, smarting.

Burns turned and saw the driver grab al-Hakim by his shoulders, throwing him up against the wall. The driver snatched the pendant from al-Hakim and ran back towards the SUV.

Burns rubbed his hurting hand and chased after the driver, al-Hakim jogging after them.

Burns caught up to the driver just as he reached the SUV. As the driver tried to get into it, Burns grabbed him by the seat of his pants, yanked him out and threw him up against the SUV.

A crowd of spectators had now gathered. The man in the car stuck behind the SUV jumped out and punched at the air saying, "Yeah! Give 'im bloody hell, mate!"

Burns wrestled with the driver who dropped the necklace onto the ground. Burns kneed him in the groin and gave him an uppercut punch. The driver crumpled over and fell to his knees.

Al-Hakim rushed over and picked up the pendant.

"Who're you working for?" Burns said in Arabic to the driver, shaking him by his shoulders. The driver did not respond, his head drooping. Burns released him and stepped back, looking around at all the gathering spectators.

"We have to get out of here," he said to al-Hakim, picking up his backpack. "These drivers nowadays," he hollered to the crowd as he backed away from the scene. "No driving etiquette. It's almost as bad as the States." He took al-Hakim by the arm and led him off.

"Should we not wait for the police?" al-Hakim said, panting from the event.

"And say what? These men were sent by imams to steal the Prophet's wife's long lost necklace? After they locked us up for being crazy, they'll confiscate the necklace as evidence."

"I hope you know what you are doing."

"Trust me." Burns led him up Saint Andrew's Street. They turned down Christ's Lane and zigzagged over to the archaeology department.

"Who do you think those men were?" al-Hakim said, out of breath as they entered the archaeology department at a fast pace.

"Specifically? I have no idea. They clearly want that." He pointed to the necklace hanging in al-Hakim's hand.

They entered an office and found Professor Umbridge sitting behind his desk working on his computer. Umbridge, a thin and well-kept man in his seventies, had no hair and a pencil-thin mustache. The day he retired would be the day he died. "Jonathan," al-Hakim said.

"Ahmed. What can I do for you?"

"Please may I introduce to you to my friend, Professor Patrick Burns, from Claremont College in California?"

"Nice to meet you," Burns said.

"The pleasure's all mine, Professor." Umbridge stood, and Burns shook his hand. "Please sit," Umbridge said, waving to the chairs in front of his desk.

"May I ask a favor of you?" al-Hakim said, sitting down next to Burns.

"Of course."

"This necklace and pendant. Patrick and I are working on identifying them for research we are doing." He handed them to Umbridge. "Could you take a look and perhaps tell us what you think as to the age and origin?"

Umbridge studied the pendant first, turning it over and back again. "Hm." He pulled out a magnifying monocle from his desk drawer and inserted it into his right eye socket. "I should say," he said in a thick British accent. "Astonishing." Turning it over, he studied it some more.

Burns and Al-Hakim waited patiently.

"Incredible," Umbridge said. "This is beyond belief." He next studied the necklace, running it up and down through his fingers. "Extraordinary." Finally, he took his monocle out and looked up at the two men. "The pendant is definitely Arabic, bronze, 7th century perhaps, the necklace, Yemenite Beads. I should say its characteristics suggest it was made between the years 600 and 900 CE." Umbridge put his monocle back up to his eye and studied the pendant again.

"What is it, Jonathan?" al-Hakim said.

"*A'isha, Umm al-mu'minin*," Umbridge said, reading from the pendant.

Al-Hakim glanced at Burns who raised his eyebrows and nodded in agreement. Umbridge leaned back in his chair and caught his breath, dropping the monocle back into his hand. "It indicates this may have belonged to A'isha, Muhammad's most influential and favorite wife. But you already know this."

"Yes," al-Hakim said. He leaned in closer to Umbridge. "We must be cautious, Jonathan. We have to unravel the puzzle of this pendant before it is made public."

"I understand, Ahmed. You have a serious discovery here. What this could do for history is significant." He handed the necklace back to al-Hakim. "I am certain of its date," Umbridge continued. "The necklace was made somewhere in Arabia around the time I propose. The artisanship well suggests it was made at that time using existing technique. The pendant was made in Mesopotamia, or perhaps Arabia, around the same time." He paused, and said, "I know of the Incident of the Necklace, relating to A'isha. This necklace appears exactly as it is described in Islamic texts."

"That is precisely what I had concluded," al-Hakim said.

"I am also certain the pendant refers to something suppressed by Bakr, but you know this as well." Umbridge paused again and calculated the two men sitting across the desk from him. "I am certain of what I have said. Based on what I can see, I believe it is indeed A'isha's necklace, from the Incident of the Necklace. You have quite a significant find and a monumental task before you. God only knows there may be men who would kill to get this from you."

"We understand that sentiment very well," al-Hakim said, glancing at Burns. He turned back to Umbridge. "Please do not discuss this with anyone, Jonathan, until we can decode it and go where it may lead us."

"You have my word, gentleman," Umbridge said.

Burns stood and shook Umbridge's hand. "Pleased to meet you, Professor. Thank you."

"You too, Professor," Umbridge said.

They departed Umbridge's office. "You had better hold on to this," al-Hakim said.

"Right."

Al-Hakim handed him the necklace. He put it around his neck, stuffing the pendant down his shirt. They departed the university.

Chapter Thirteen

The three great pyramids and Sphinx of Giza stood awash in the hazy afternoon Egyptian sun. Many Egyptologists had dedicated their lives over the past two centuries to studying the archaeology, structure, history, purpose and symbolism of the great pyramids. To Abdullah Nasir Yassim, who walked down *Shari Et Tahrir* street in their midst, they were just a symbol to a misguided and polytheistic past. He scoffed at the British, Americans, French and Germans who wasted their lives day in and day out trying to learn of this past. To him, there was no need. All one needed was Allah and his word. There was no need to know anything else.

He passed a dirty canal and stepped over garbage strewn on the street. A man slapped a camel on its ass with a crop as it passed by. Yassim noticed a tour bus carrying European tourists zipping past him. He sneered at them as the bus spewed out its black exhaust. An older couple sitting on the bus gawked at him from their open window. *Infidels*, he stewed.

He turned and went into a small, dilapidated apartment building. Dirty, broken down, yet several Egyptian families lived there in squalor. He climbed the broken stairs and entered an apartment on the third floor where three other men waited for him. They were dressed in *Galabias* and each had long beards like his. Standing to greet him, they each wore their *Tagiyah*, a white knitted skullcap. A young man with a long beard and in his middle twenties stood near the door. Yassim nodded at him, and the young man departed the room and closed the door, standing guard just outside. "Sit, my brothers," Yassim said. He sat on a torn, dirty sofa.

The men sat on a hard wooden bench opposite him. One man, all of twenty-five years, who had a missing right ear, studied Yassim intently. The other man was in his fifties and had a tired, sun-parched and leathery face. "I have disturbing news," Yassim said. "Our brothers in England were thwarted in their task of obtaining A'isha's necklace."

The old man rocked forward, his long face losing color. The young man with the missing right ear sat upright and grimaced.

"But alas," Yassim continued, raising his hand slightly, "I have instructed them to take more intense measures. They are contacting our sources there to obtain weapons that can aide in their pursuit. If they must kill these infidels to obtain the necklace, if that is what Allah, the compassionate, the merciful, wishes, then so be it." He fidgeted in his seat. "I have no doubt we will be successful in our endeavors, as Allah has commanded."

"Yes," said the older man.

"We will," said the man with the missing ear. "I am ready to do my part."

"Yes, I know of this," Yassim said. "You are most loyal and trustworthy, Nazim."

Yassim dismissed his deputies and retired to his room where he sat on a mat and read his *Qur'an*. A veiled woman brought him a cool, mint tea, *shai bi-nana*. He waved her away.

A younger Fatima Burns rested in a hospital bed. Exhausted, she smiled at her husband, dressed in scrubs, as he entered the room carrying a baby in a swaddling blanket. He handed her the baby and sat down beside her. "Sara Nafi'a Burns," she said to him.

"What a name," he said, running his fingers through her hair.

She gently kissed her daughter on the forehead. "She is so beautiful, Patrick."

"Just like her mother," he said.

"As Allah is my witness," Fatima said. "I love you so much."

Burns leaned down and kissed his wife. "I love you, too." He then kissed his new baby daughter.

Burns snapped out of his daydream as a city bus pulled up and stopped in front of him and al-Hakim as they sat waiting at a bus stop on Drummer Street.

They boarded the bus and sat near the front. Burns glanced up when a young Arabic man boarded the bus after them. The man averted his eyes so as not draw attention to himself.

The young man stood in the back of the bus. Resembling a young professor, he wore causal Dockers and a tweed jacket. Clean-shaven, he carried no books or book bag, however.

A few miles later, the bus stopped outside al-Hakim's flat. Burns and al-Hakim got off, Burns watching as the man followed and walked slowly down the street in the opposite direction. They entered the building and went up to the flat.

After Burns and al-Hakim had entered the flat, the young man doubled back across the street where he stood and surveilled the building.

Chapter Fourteen

Inside al-Hakim's flat, Burns helped put everything back in order. "They were clearly on to you even before I arrived," Burns said.

"How could this get out so fast? And to know of our connection, Patrick?"

"There must be double-operatives within the American operations in Iraq. We cannot trust anyone on that end. My contact was very clear." He helped him straighten the askew kitchen table and also picked up the papers from the floor. After they had straightened everything, Burns pulled the necklace from around his neck. "Can you imagine," he said, "that this could have been A'isha's? And here I am wearing it?"

"Many in the Muslim world would think it sacrilegious for a Catholic to wear that necklace. Some cleric would issue a fatwā calling for your death."

Burns nodded and said, "Yeah, great. Thanks."

Al-Hakim smiled at him and pulled out two small spiral notebooks from a nearby desk, slid one to Burns across the table, and kept the other one. "Now," al-Hakim said, "shall we decipher this pendant?"

The man across the street hid in a stairwell, waited and watched. When pedestrians approached, he ducked out of sight. After they passed, he stepped out of the shadows to peer at the lighted flat on the second floor across the street. He watched the building closely. The building had four floors, and had been built in the nineteen fifties, or sometime after the war. It had two flats on each floor, one on each side of the stairwell. The flats went the length of the building from front to back so each flat on each floor had the living room window facing out onto the street in front.

He looked up and down the street and scurried over to read the register next to the building. He found al-Hakim's name and flat number, 2a.

He hurried back across the street and assumed his post where he continued to watch the flat. He pulled from his pocket a handgun, examined it, and replaced it in his pocket. He rocked up and down on his heels.

Al-Hakim opened the drawer to a nearby bureau and pulled out a loupe. "Okay," he said. "This should help." He put the loupe up to his right eye and examined the pendant. The first inscription he read, in Arabic:

كر انتقل الى رحمة الله تعالى لكن الصُفّة تظهر

He transcribed the words in Arabic on his pad and translated them into English, "Bakr went to the mercy of Allah, yet the *Suffah* shows."

"A'isha's father, the first *caliph*," Burns said thinking aloud. He jotted this passage down in his notepad.

"And we know Bakr was Muhammad's closest confidant, besides A'isha," al-Hakim said, also thinking aloud. "And they both were responsible for interpreting many of Muhammad's dreams and visions, even writing down many of the collections of *ahādīth*."

"And the *Suffah* was the shaded platform area where Muhammad used to lead prayer." Burns spoke to jog his memory, not to lecture al-Hakim. He wrote *Suffah* on his pad and circled it several times. He tapped his pencil.

"Which was within the *Al-Masjid al-Nabawi*," al-Hakim said.

"The second holiest mosque in Islam containing the tombs of both Muhammad and Bakr," Burns said.

Al-Hakim continued studying the pendant. "And this," he said in Arabic:

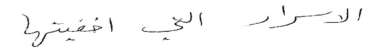

"The secrets thee hath concealed," Burns said.

"Yes." Al-Hakim glanced up at him.

"That must mean the excluded *ḥadīth*."

"Perhaps," al-Hakim said. "But where does this *ḥadīth* rest, or with whom?"

"If it rests with Bakr we'll never get at it." Burns thought a moment. "And, if it rests under the *Suffah*, we'll never get at it either."

"Most certainly. The Saudis would never allow this." Al-Hakim tapped his pencil on his lips and studied his notes. "Bakr went to the mercy of Allah, yet the *Suffah* shows, the secrets thee hath concealed."

"The *Suffah*," Burns said, "which is near Bakr's grave, must reveal the secrets, or where this *ḥadīth* must be, because A'isha couldn't have buried it under the *Suffah* or in her father's tomb."

Al-Hakim nodded. "And the final inscription that reads:"

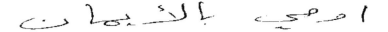

"Faith inspired it," he said in English after writing it in Arabic on his notebook.

"I don't like the sound of that," Burns said, shifting in his seat.

"And," al-Hakim continued, "the first inscription, *A'isha, Umm al-mu'minin.*"

"The Mother of the Believers," said Burns.

"You see the way it is positioned on top," al-Hakim said, pointing to the spot so Burns could see, "like it is a title, or shows ownership?"

عائشة ام المؤمنين

"I thought about that. The line underneath, though shorter in length, does set it apart from the rest and underscores as to who it belonged to."

"Precisely. Yes, well, let us review." Al-Hakim underlined each passage in his notebook and said, "*Umm al-mu'minin*, which is the first one at the top, set apart from the rest, as if a title showing ownership, and Bakr went to the mercy of Allah, yet the *Suffah* shows, the secrets thee hath concealed and faith inspired it. Okay, now," he said, continuing, turning the pendant over. "The markings are next." He scratched his forehead. "This one here, look closely, Patrick." He handed him the pendant and the loupe.

Using the loupe, Burns studied the tiny depictions. "Trees, bunched tightly together, with the sun overhead."

"You are thinking what I am thinking?"

Burns nodded at him. "I know what this is," Burns said. "The *Jannat al-Baqi*. The tree garden of heaven. Muhammad blessed it whenever he passed by."

"Yes, the cemetery in *Medina* where many of Muhammad's relatives and companions are buried, including his wives, most notably, A'isha."

"The sun over the trees symbolizing heaven," Burns said.

"Yes." Al-Hakim frowned.

"What is it, Ahmed?"

"The clues she may have left at both locations, assuming she did, may no longer be there because much of *Al-Masjid al-Nabawi* has been rebuilt many times over the centuries and *Jannat al-Baqi* has been altered, most notably after *Ibn Saud* had much of the tomb markings destroyed to prevent pilgrims from worshiping at the graves."

"Well," Burns said, "hopefully we can find illustrations in libraries from the time of A'isha to follow her clues."

Al-Hakim nodded. "Perhaps, yes, but I doubt any maps or illustrations will depict clues she left there. Most certainly we can ascertain where the graves had been, and as I have been there, as I know you have, we do have some frame of reference, but there are no markings there any longer."

Burns examined the pendant again. "And this, the next engraving, a small rectangle with circles on its corners."

"Well," said al-Hakim. "I think that might be the original, *Suffah*, *Al-Masjid al-Nabawi*, and the circles the location of the original date palms. Although it is slightly askew, pointing in a northwest direction because the original mosque pointed that way."

"Yes," said Burns. "And as we know, the *Suffah* was inside the *Al-Masjid al-Nabawi* and the *Qiblah* was originally in the direction of *Jerusalem*, which was northwest of *Medina*. Perhaps this is meant to signify the direction of the original *Qiblah* and the *Suffah* area within the original mosque, pointing in a northwesterly direction, towards *Jerusalem*."

"Perhaps," al-Hakim said, biting his lip.

"Possibly this *ḥadīth* is buried in *Jerusalem*?"

"Yes," al-Hakim said. "We know it could not be buried at either *Al-Masjid al-Nabawi* or *Jannat al-Baqi*. Although A'isha did live out her life there in *Medina*. It could be in *Jerusalem*, but we have this clue pointing us to *Jannat al-Baqi*."

"She must have placed a clue there. But what would we be looking for if the markers are all gone?"

"We will have to match photos," al-Hakim said. "Many were taken before the Saudis destroyed the markers."

Burns passed the pendant to al-Hakim who scrutinized the pendant again for the longest time. "This last image," he said. "What do you make of it, Patrick?" He passed the pendant and the loupe back to him.

"It's obviously the depiction of a person sitting on the back of a camel."

"Yes," al-Hakim said.

"And a woman at that, on the back of a camel?" Burns dropped the loupe from his eye into his hand. He shot a glance at al-Hakim. "A'isha?"

"Although she would have been on a howdah, most likely an enclosed one."

Burns stared at the woman on the back of the camel. "Perhaps it was too complicated to chisel onto this small pendant, and the fact that you wouldn't be able to see it was a woman. I think if you look closely you can make out that is depicting a woman."

"Perhaps, because she was an educated and liberated woman of her time, she rode like that."

"If this is all true," Burns said, tapping his finger on the pendant, "I wonder if this depiction of herself on the back of a camel is somehow connected with The Battle of the Camel, because this was an integral event in the history of Islam."

Al-Hakim nodded and stroked his grey beard. "It is peculiar why she would place this depiction of herself in such a way. It would have no significance otherwise. Why show herself on the back of a camel?" He paused, and said, "She wanted whoever found this to contemplate exactly this question, why she would depict herself on the back of a camel."

"If not to draw attention to a woman on the back of a camel," Burns said. "The camel is significant."

"And because she was a major figure in The Battle of The Camel, commanding the battle from the back of a camel, and this is a momentous historical event in Islamic history, as you said, this might be what she is alluding to, herself on the back of the camel to show her commanding the battle in The Battle of The Camel."

"It has to be," Burns said.

The two men sat silently for a moment.

"What are you thinking, Patrick?"

"That the necklace was lost much earlier than the pendant could have been made, in reference to this historical event."

"Right," al-Hakim said. "The Battle of the Camel was after Muhammad's death during the struggle for power of the *Caliphate* when A'isha joined forces with Talha and Zubayr and tried to defeat Ali near *Basra*."

"And the whole exclusion of this *ḥadīth* was well after the incident of the necklace but before The Battle of the Camel."

"According to Umbridge," al-Hakim said, "the necklace is dated at about the right time. So she could have later attached the pendant to her favorite necklace."

"Conceivably." Burns appraised the pendant again.

"Okay," al-Hakim said. "Let us proceed on the assumption this *ḥadīth* survived, similar to the Dead Sea Scrolls and other archaeological finds."

"And the necklace is hers, and the pendant was later added to indicate the whereabouts of this *ḥadīth*."

"Yes." Al-Hakim closed his notebook.

"If anyone could pull this off," Burns said closing his notebook as well, "it was A'isha, who was an obviously clever woman."

"Most agreeable."

"What have we got to lose?"

"We start at the beginning," al-Hakim said. "The *Suffah* obviously is the first clue. We should scour the mosque. The reference to the *Suffah* is a symbolic feature within the mosque, alluding to the original direction of the *Qiblah*, towards *Jerusalem*."

"Right," Burns said. "These etchings and enigmatic sayings on the pendant she set up are not meant to be easy to decipher. We could be wrong in our extrapolations."

The Lost *Hadīth*

"Like all hypotheses," al-Hakim said while packing his backpack, "we test our hypothesis, Patrick. First, we need to find illustrations, pictures and maps of the two locations in *Medina* from the time of Muhammad and A'isha at the university, then go to *Medina*."

"We most certainly will need pictures of the grave markers at *Jannat al-Baqi*," Burns said, putting the necklace around his neck and stuffing the pendant down inside his shirt where it came to rest against his chest. They finished gathering up their notes, packed up and hurried down the stairs.

The man across the street watched them depart. He saw Burns carrying his satchel and backpack, and al-Hakim who carried a large backpack. They stopped and waited at the bus stop.

The streetlights dimly illuminated the area this evening. The man darted across the street, heading right for them, pulling the handgun from under his jacket.

"He's got a gun!" someone shouted. Pedestrians started screaming and scattering.

The man lost his element of surprise and started shooting at the two men.

Three bullets whizzed past Burns and al-Hakim and embedded into the building behind them. Burns' military training kicked in as he grabbed al-Hakim and dropped down behind the bus stop bench. The man rushed forward and pumped off four more rounds into the bench.

Burns threw his backpack at the man just as he came upon them. The backpack distracted the attacker, as he had to use his other hand to deflect it. This allowed Burns the opportunity to roll out from behind the bench and kick the man's legs out from under him. The man fell sideways and fired three more shots into the air. Burns grabbed the man's hand that held the gun.

The man would not let go. Burns struggled to wrench the gun from him. The man squeezed off two more rounds into the air, hitting the top floor apartment behind them.

They continued struggling, the gun flailing.

Al-Hakim jumped up and found the cover to a nearby trashcan.

The man squeezed the trigger again, but the gun only clicked.

Al-Hakim smashed the trashcan lid down onto the man's head repeatedly until Burns gained the upper hand and overcame him. He kicked the man in the face. The man fell onto the street unconscious.

Burns grabbed the gun and stuffed it under his shirt between his belt and abdomen. He pulled his shirt down over it. "Let's get out of here," he said to al-Hakim.

They ran down the street and around the corner where Burns pulled out the gun, wiped it down with his shirt, and dropped it into a large trash bin behind a restaurant.

They made their way over to the next street where they found a bus pulling up at another bus stop. They got on and the bus pulled away. They had to take a roundabout bus route back to the university.

The libraries and study halls at Cambridge stayed open late for students who had to cram for either research papers or exams. There, they found old maps and some pictures of the grave markers at the *Jannat al-Baqi*. They found some pictures of A'isha's headstone taken before the Saudis took control of Arabia. They scanned the photos of the headstone using his loupe and discovered some etchings. They made copies of everything they found.

Burns stuffed the copies into his leather satchel. He and al-Hakim headed to the train station and back to London where they waited for a flight at Heathrow that would take them to *Medina, Saudi Arabia*.

The two men who had attacked al-Hakim and Burns earlier near the university turned the corner to al-Hakim's street. They couldn't get close to the flat because of police activity.

The passenger, who had a large, swollen black eye from his beating earlier with Burns, banged his hand onto the steering wheel. He shook his head, looked over at his accomplice, backed up the street, turned around and drove off.

Chapter Fifteen

A Mercedes sedan pulled out and followed Cunningham's SUV near the entrance to the Green Zone.

Three security guards accompanied him, driving hell-bent along the *Matar Sadam Al Duwali* Road, or Airport road. It ran from the Green Zone to Baghdad International Airport. It could have been five miles of small arms fire, IEDs, or rocket propelled grenades, but the security had significantly improved over the last couple of years.

Inside, the major reviewed files on his cast of characters.

The sedan following him tailed at a close distance.

Up ahead a van moved into the flow of traffic where it came to a complete stop blocking traffic.

Cunningham noticed the slowing vehicles ahead. The SUV had no choice but to slow, coming to a complete stop.

The sedan stopped behind the GMC, blocking it from backing up and turning around.

Without warning, four masked men sporting AK-47s burst out of the van and swarmed Cunningham's vehicle.

Two men, one next to the driver's door and the other next to the passenger's, slapped devices to each door.

The SUV driver jammed it into reverse. Its tires squealed and black rubber smoke plumed out of the wheel wells. The SUV slammed into the sedan behind them.

The driver struggled to put the SUV into drive as the devices on the doors exploded, blowing the the doors off. The SUV jolted to the right and spun around, the driver and the security guard in the passenger's seat knocked unconscious.

Two men jumped out of the sedan and stormed Cunningham's vehicle. They shot the driver and the guard in the passenger's seat. The guard in the back seat opened fire and blasted two of the assailants, killing them both. One of the remaining assailants returned fire and killed the bodyguard in the back seat.

The masked men pulled open the back doors on either side. One man grabbed Cunningham while another placed a black hood over his head. They hustled him into the van and sped away.

One of the men from the sedan gathered together Cunningham's files and his briefcase. He and his accomplice jumped back into the sedan and sped off.

They disembarked from their Saudi Airlines flight at the *Prince Mohammad Bin Abdulaziz* International Airport in *Medina*. Burns hailed a taxi.

On the way to the Hotel International, they stopped at a men's clothing store and bought traditional Saudi Arabian garb including a *Thobe*, a *Tagiyah*, and to place over the *Tagiyah* each bought a *Ghutra*, a red and white checkered square scarf made of cotton, folded into a triangle. Finally, each bought an *Agal*, a thick, double black cord worn on top of the *Ghutra* to hold it into place.

They checked into a room at the extravagant and ornate hotel, which catered to mostly business travelers and tourists. Al-Hakim freshened up in the bathroom while Burns opened up and spread out on a table an ancient map of the *Jannat al-Baqi* cemetery and another early map of the *Al-Masjid al-Nabawi* Mosque on the bed. He closely studied the maps and made markings and notations on them.

Several minutes later, al-Hakim came out of the bathroom drying his face, wearing boxer shorts. "What do you think, Patrick?"

"How much they have changed since the time of Muhammad."

The Lost *Hadīth*

Al-Hakim dressed into his Saudi garb as Burns took a shower.

A few minutes later, Burns came from the bathroom, and he, too, dressed as a Saudi. Al-Hakim sat studying the maps. "And your impression, Ahmad?"

"Well," he said, "I think there is much here that will allow us to begin."

"I agree." They packed up the maps and pictures and departed the hotel. They arrived by taxi at *Al-Masjid al-Nabawi*, the Mosque of the Prophet, several minutes later and stood outside admiring the structure. It was gigantic, ornate, and exquisite, all its Arabic architecture and design shining.

They had been here before, but it was still quite a sight to see the second holiest mosque in Islam. Muhammad had built the original mosque next to his house. The original mosque was now within a larger mosque built around it over the centuries, most notably by the Ottoman Turks, then later by the Saudis. The current mosque had several minarets built with lavishly decorated polychrome marble and stones. The columns were made of white marble and brass hubs supporting pointed arches built of black and white stones.

They went inside and made their way over to where the location of the original mosque and *Suffah* had been. The area little resembled the original *Suffah* and mosque from the time of Muhammad. "Well," al-Hakim said, "we know the original *Qiblah* pointed northwest towards *Jerusalem*, or more precisely the *al-haram al-qudsī ash-sharīf*, before it was redesigned to point towards *Mecca*.

"Yes," Burns said, scanning the area. "According to testimony from his companions, Muhammad was leading a prayer at the *Masjid al-Qiblatain* when he received a revelation from Allah telling him to turn towards the *Masjid al Haram*, the *Ka'aba* in *Mecca* as the *Qiblah*."

"Right, the revelation of *Surat al-Baqara*," al-Hakim said, scanning the large room too.

"So," Burns said, "the marking resembling the original *Al-Masjid al-Nabawi* on the pendant seems to point in the original direction, towards *Jerusalem*, to where the *Qiblah* had pointed." He walked over to the exact spot where the original *Suffah* had been. Al-Hakim joined him and examined the location.

"Even though I have been here before," Burns said, sighing, "it still takes my breath away. I mean, right here, at this exact spot, is where

Muhammad preached."

"I know," al-Hakim said. "If only we could figure out time travel and be that fly on the wall." Burns smiled and nodded. Al-Hakim turned to look south towards *Mecca*, then northwest towards *Jerusalem*.

"What is it, Ahmed?"

"Let us go to Bakr's tomb."

They made their way to Bakr's tomb, which rested near Muhammad's, and stood gazing at Bakr's tomb.

Burns examined Bakr's tomb, then Muhammad's, appreciating the sacred significance of this site. He looked over at al-Hakim and nodded. Burns respected the fact that over a billion people living today followed this man's teachings. After all, this man, on orders from Allah, started a religion, or as some contend, built upon the other two religions. Burns studied Bakr's tomb again. An ornate gate guarded it. It had a hole in the gate that one could peer through to see the tomb.

Al-Hakim looked through the hole and studied it. "Abu Bakr lies here," al-Hakim said, reading from a gold plate on the door.

Burns analyzed the writings on the pendant. "Hum, yes," he said, "yet the *Suffah* shows." He searched around for clues. Nothing. He reinserted the pendant down between his chest and his *Thobe*.

"Let us think," al-Hakim said, pulling away after peeking through the hole into Bakr's tomb. "We know the *Suffah* was the shaded spot from which Muhammad stood and preached. It was where his followers prayed. So, it revealed Muhammad teaching the word of Allah."

"But now shows, or reveals, the secrets A'isha has written?" Burns inspected his notes. He tried to think his way through the clues they had found thus far to try to dislodge something he may be missing.

"Yes, Patrick," al-Hakim said. "The secret truly lies with A'isha, not Bakr. He rests with Allah, but his secrets, or A'isha's, are revealed by the original *Suffah*, inside the original mosque. I think the *Suffah* is an allegorical reference and the marking depicting the original *Al-Masjid al-Nabawi* directs us on towards *Jerusalem*."

"I agree," Burns said, thinking aloud. "Because Muhammad preached from the original *Suffah*, it now reveals or points us on to where she has hidden this *ḥādīth*."

Burns knelt down next to the tomb. "Look at this depiction," he said, pointing to a simple, one-inch long engraving down near the bottom of the gate and off to one side. It appeared someone had etched it a while ago because it seemed to have been polished over in an effort to get rid or obscure it. He saw a diminutive rectangle, superimposed circles drawn over each of the corners. Within the rectangle, a man stood, but his face had no features.

Al-Hakim had to get close to see the marking. "Muhammad," he said.

Burns looked again, this time more closely, the loupe in his eye. He stood up next to al-Hakim and thought about what they had found. A security guard hovered nearby. Burns spoke Arabic fluently and knew all there was to know concerning Islam so he could pass for a Muslim if he needed to, despite being an American, or rather, a Canadian.

The guard passed by and strode off.

Burns duplicated the depiction in his notebook. On the right side next to the rectangle was a marking. The rectangle was askew, not quite up and down, but tilted slightly to the left. "That could be a directional pointer, pointing north," Burns said, tapping his finger on his replication.

"Please let me see the pendant again," al-Hakim said.

Burns pulled it from around his neck and passed it to him.

"The rectangle on the pendant is the same as the one we see here," said al-Hakim, "minus the directional arrow and Muhammad in the center of it." He handed the pendant back to Burns who once again stuffed it down his *Thobe*.

"Okay," Burns said. "So the rectangle depicts the original *Al-Masjid al-Nabawi* and it is pointing towards *Jerusalem* as the original *Qiblah*. There's a directional symbol pointing north so when one looks at it he will see the tilt of the rectangle is meant that way."

"Yes, and the circles mean they were the original date palms. Come."

Burns followed him back to the location to where the original *Al-Masjid al-Nabawi* had been. They stood there admiring the columns, each having historical significance and sayings on them. The columns marked the spot of the original corners of the mosque. The replica columns now before them had been built much later. The original *Suffah* had been an open-air area within the mosque and had a raised platform for reading the *Qur'an*. This was where Muhammad and his followers performed the *Salat* facing towards *Jerusalem*. The original mosque was a rectangular enclosure of thirty meters by thirty-five meters, built around palm trunks and mud walls.

Burns pulled out of his leather satchel a photocopied sketch of the original mosque in the time of Muhammad. He orientated it as best he could in relation to their position.

"Bakr went to the mercy of Allah, yet the *Suffah* shows," al-Hakim said, thinking aloud. "So, allegorically, the *Suffah*, and therein the original *Qiblah*, inside the original *Al-Masjid al-Nabawi,* is pointing us in the direction where A'isha has hidden what it is Bakr has forbidden."

"Or more clues to where A'isha has hidden it. And what's the most sacred site there for Muslims?" Burns asked rhetorically.

"*Masjid Qubbat As-Sakhrah,"* al-Hakim said.

"Exactly. *The Dome of the Rock*," Burns said, making a notation in his notebook. He withdrew his U.S. military issue lensatic compass from his satchel, stood at the base of where the *Suffah* had been and, using a regional map, calculated the azimuth in the direction where it pointed, *Jerusalem*. He made a notation of the azimuth in his notebook.

"Okay," al-Hakim said, thinking aloud again, "we know Bakr, upon Muhammad's death assumed power and solidified the faith and chose which of the *aḥādīth* to include, and which ones to exclude, although *Shiite* Muslims dispute much of any of this attributed to both him and his daughter."

"Yes," Burns said, glancing over his shoulder at the religious police walking past them.

"Therefore," al-Hakim continued, "he is with Allah, as A'isha asserts, but the *Suffah*, inside the original mosque reveals, because of A'isha's clues, where to find the *ḥadīth* is that he had excluded."

"I agree."

"And remember, Patrick, clever woman that she was, as one of Muhammad's most significant confidants, if not the most important one in Muhammad's inner circle, besides Bakr and Ali, responsible for him understanding and accepting his visions from Allah, she hid this *ḥadīth* because she probably disagreed with its exclusion as she had written them and hoped one day they would be revealed."

"That's the perennial question. Reveal it for what purpose?"

Al-Hakim shook his head.

"Okay," said Burns, "let's think." He surveyed the area of the *Suffah*. "We have the pendant with the reference to the *Suffah*, and the rectangle that is a depiction of the original mosque with the circles on each corner indicating the original date palms, wherein lied the *Suffah*, and hence the *Qiblah*, which was firstly oriented towards *Jerusalem* before being changed to face *Mecca*…"

"Towards *the Dome of The Rock* in *Jerusalem*," said al-Hakim.

"Yes. But I doubt she could have had it buried there as well." Burns looked up at the large decorative ceiling. "There must be more clues there."

"Yes," al-Hakim said. "But what of *Jannat al-Baqi*?"

"There has to be a clue there," Burns said. "Let's go have a look."

Burns followed al-Hakim who took only a few short steps before coming to a quick halt at one of the columns that represented one of the original date palms, the Column of A'isha. Al-Hakim smiled. "Like we have said, Patrick, clever woman."

Burns smiled too, then followed al-Hakim toward the southern extension and out through the Gate of Peace.

Chapter Sixteen

Cunningham, sitting in a wooden chair in the center of the small room where Zamin al-Hayali had been tortured and shot earlier, slumped forward. Through a loosely fitted black hood that covered his head, he could see stains of dried blood on the floor at his feet and a bloodstained wall to his right side. With his hands tied behind his back and his legs bound to the chair, a dimly lit dangling light bulb hung over his head.

The door to the room opened, someone entered and took the hood off. He peered up at al-Salah standing in front of him, a younger man holding a wooden club standing beside him. The young man threw the hood on the floor at his feet. "Do you know who I am, Major?"

He nodded.

"Then you know I have the power and grace to set you free." Al-Salah slowly circled him.

Cunningham did not answer, but stared straight ahead.

"I only am interested in retrieving the necklace that rightfully belongs to the Iraqi people."

Cunningham still did not answer.

Al-Salah stopped behind Cunningham, bent down and whispered in his ear. "You see, Major, it has no value to you Americans."

Cunningham said nothing.

Al-Salah walked around to face him, Cunningham staring straight ahead, almost through him. "Did you see it, Major?" Al-Salah cocked his head, raised his eyebrow and waited for an answer.

Nothing. No answer. Al-Salah nodded to his torturer. The man stepped forward and clubbed Cunningham across his face. Blood and saliva splattered out onto the floor at al-Salah's feet. "Did you not understand the question, Major? Did you see the necklace?"

Cunningham said nothing, but spit blood out and onto the floor near al-Salah's foot. Al-Salah signaled again to his torturer.

"I did," Cunningham said through the pain.

The torturer lowered his club.

"It's a mystery as to what it means," Cunningham said.

"Ah, but it should be my mystery." Al-Salah raised his index finger and squinted at Cunningham, his mouth curling into a smug grin. "You see, major..."

"I'm afraid that's not to be," Cunningham said.

Al-Salah's grin disappeared. He lowered his finger, backed up and waved his hand at his henchman who stepped forward and again clubbed Cunningham across the face.

After a moment, Cunningham straightened his head and said to the thug, "May Allah have mercy on your soul." He spit out a bloodied tooth onto al-Salah's shoe. He glared up at al-Salah and said, "But not yours."

Al-Salah shook the tooth from his shoe. The torturer looked at al-Salah who nodded back at him. The torturer clubbed Cunningham again, his head falling forward, bloody saliva dribbled down his chin and dripped onto the floor.

"You know, Major, this mission you have sent this Professor Burns on is a dangerous one."

He did not answer again.

Al-Salah snapped. "You have no idea how this could lead to chaos, war perhaps."

"So...you...admit...its...significance?" Cunningham breathed slowly, struggling to get the words out. "And, you...think...it...would be...best in...your hands than...in the hands...of scholars?"

"Depends on whose scholars."

Cunningham cleared his throat. He regained some of his ability to speed up his speech, but not at a normal clip. "Look, you can torture me...all you want, but these operations...are blind." He spit out some more bloody saliva. It too splattered onto al-Salah's shoe.

Al-Salah glanced at his shoe. He moved back two steps and sighed. "I am tiring of your attitude, Major. I have the power to spare your life, and the life of this Professor Burns."

"You really expect me to…believe that? Look, I have no idea where…Burns is, or what he knows. It could be months…before I hear from him."

"And you expect me to believe that? You see, I am a patient man. We have waited for more than a thousand years to obtain the necklace and prevent it from exposing this false *ḥadīth*, if it does indeed exist. A few more weeks or months, as you say, will not matter." He turned to go.

"You will not succeed," Cunningham said, raising his head to glare at him.

Al-Salah took the bait and stopped to listen.

"Burns is an authority on the matter and he'll find this *ḥadīth*. You'll never get your bloody hands on it."

Al-Salah never turned to look back at Cunningham. He opened the door and walked out. His torturer followed and turned out the light, shutting the door behind him. Cunningham dropped his head into his chest.

Outside on the Sadr City street, al-Salah's large, black and heavily guarded Mercedes SUV, waited. Just before getting into it, he said to Tahseen Omar-Hamed, a short Iraqi man dressed in Armani slacks, a Polo shirt and sport coat who waited there, "My patience is waning. Find this Burns. Get the necklace, and kill him. We have no more time to waste."

Al-Salah climbed into his vehicle. Hamed put on his Armani sunglasses and jumped into a black Mercedes sedan parked behind al-Salah's SUV. Both vehicles sped away.

Chapter Seventeen

The man who shot at al-Hakim and Burns on the street near al-Hakim's flat in Cambridge answered his ringing mobile phone at Heathrow Airport, his face swollen from being kicked by Burns. "They have flown to *Medina*," he said into his phone.

Hamed, on the other end said, "Go to *Medina* and follow them. I have operatives there who can provide information. I will arrive shortly."

The man closed his phone and approached the ticketing agent at the counter for Saudi Airlines.

Burns followed al-Hakim out of the *Al-Masjid al-Nabawi* and across the way to *Jannat al-Baqi*. They entered through the main gate and walked along the path where many pilgrims meandered. They passed the site where Muhammad's daughters were buried and the graves of Muhammad's wives, including A'isha's.

Burns pulled from his satchel the pictures and map of the cemetery taken during the time of the Ottoman Empire. He took care not to draw attention because Saudi authorities would confiscate their maps and pictures and perhaps prosecute them because the *Wahhabi* interpretations of Islam forbade worshiping at any grave. Although they were not worshiping, the items they carried would suggest they might be, or complicate matters.

Burns orientated the map to where they stood. Many of the markings on the graves and tombs had been destroyed over the years, most notably after 1925 when the Saudi *Wahhabis* took control from the ashes of the Ottoman Empire and established in Arabia, the Royal Kingdom of Saudi Arabia.

Burns took the loupe and scanned one of the pictures. The illustration showed the positions of the tombs and the headstones before the markings were destroyed.

"This is exactly where A'isha's grave should be," Burns said pointing to a grave nearby. Al-Hakim reflected in silence for a moment so Burns did the same.

"Even though I was raised a *Shiite*," al-Hakim said, "I still show respect to his most favorite and revered wife."

Burns used the loupe and closely examined another photograph of A'isha's grave, its marker intact before the *Wahhabis* destroyed it.

"What it is, Patrick?"

"It's very difficult to see, but I can just make it out. I think I see the same depiction of the woman on the back of the camel on the tomb marker as it is appears on the pendant. Here, look." He handed the photo and loupe to al-Hakim.

The Lost *Hadīth*

Al-Hakim examined the photo. "Yes," he said. "I see it. However, there are two directional arrows on this depiction. One is a directional arrow pointing due north, and one points in a northeasterly direction next to the camel." He handed the photo back to Burns.

Examining it again he said, "Yes, you're right. We need to line up the picture with the location of the original headstone." He reoriented himself facing in the same direction he figured the headstone had been.

Al-Hakim spotted two Saudi police officers approaching on the path from the direction of Abdullah Al Tayeb, one of Muhammad's son's, grave. "Hurry, Patrick. Policemen."

Burns used his compass and placed it over the picture. He aligned true north first, because most likely that would be what had been used back then, not magnetic north. True north was marked in the sky by the north celestial pole, normally the position of Polaris. He then aligned the compass's needle in the direction the northeasterly arrow pointed. He rechecked that he had closely aligned himself in the direction of the original headstone. In his notebook, he recorded the azimuth at forty-eight degrees.

Al-Hakim moved in close to Burns and took the picture from him. He folded and stuffed it in his pocket and motioned with his head in the direction of the two police officers passing by on the walkway. The officers glanced in their direction and meandered up the path.

After the officers had passed, Burns took the picture from

al-Hakim. He pulled a map of the region out of his satchel and aligned it under the map of the cemetery. Using his compass as a straight edge, he drew a pencil line out from the direction of the cemetery using the azimuth he had just recorded. He extended the line across the regional map. The pencil line went straight across the desert regions of *Ha'il* and *Hudud Ash Shamaliyah* of Arabia, into the southern region of Iraq and on into Iran.

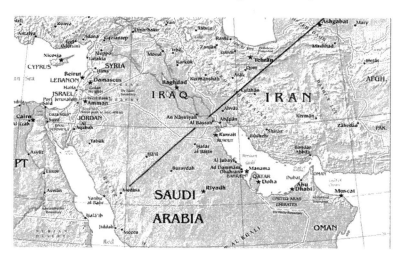

"Look at that," Burns said.

"I see," said al-Hakim. "The line crosses nothing significant until it reaches Iraq and intersects near *Basra*."

"Yes," said Burns. "Near where A'isha commanded the rebellion against Ali from the back of the camel."

"Yes, of course."

Burns folded the maps, the picture, and put them, along with his compass and pencil, in his satchel. He and al-Hakim stood there gazing out over the sandy and dusty cemetery with its broken grave markers.

"But where and what would we be looking for in *Basra*?" Burns said. "There is no concrete evidence where the Battle of the Camel actually took place. It's a vast region."

"Yes, and we know she had not actually directed the battle from *Basra*, but from the *Wadi-us-Saba,* near *Khuraiba* outside *Basra*."

"*Wadi-us-Saba,* the Valley of the Lion. I drove near there on a convoy at the start of the war."

"Okay, so we see that the line goes through the area of *Khuraiba* near the *Wadi-us-Saba*." Al-Hakim turned and faced northwest. "We have one clue that points towards *Jerusalem*," he looked that way, "or most likely the *Masjid Qubbat As-Sakhrah*, because that is most significant to Muslims, and another points us to the *Wadi-us-Saba*." He turned and pointed in that direction.

"And we know A'isha was taken off the battlefield after Ali had the legs of her camel cut off," al-Hakim continued. "Ali had ordered that she not be killed, because she had been the most significant wife of Muhammad. The litter she had been riding in had been pierced by arrows but she was lifted out and borne to a house in *Basra*."

"Yes," Burns said. "But the house in *Basra* would certainly not exist today."

"Right. Therefore, we should go to the *Masjid Qubbat As-Sakhrah* first. Perhaps there are clues there, or the *ḥadīth* itself. If not, then we should go to the university in Cairo as it has extensive documents, maps and illustrations on The Battle of the Camel, the *Wadi-us-Saba* region, and perhaps the house in *Basra*. We might be able to find a map or two that clearly shows the general location as where the Battle of the Camel took place near *Wadi-us-Saba*."

Burns nodded, and they exited the cemetery where they caught a taxicab back to the hotel.

Arabia, after *Hijra,* or 662 AD

The manservant who had placed the codices in the pottery jar on the ledge in the cave, made his way up the path he and A'isha traversed two years earlier. He led his camel along.

He tied the reins of his camel to a cotton shrubbery bush, unhooked a tool pouch tied to the camel's back and continued up the narrow path where he found the cave. He crawled into the cave and chiseled some engravings onto the walls.

Several minutes later, he shimmied back out of the cave and, using his chisel, etched more markings onto the sandstone on the area just above the cave entrance.

Around the corner from the cave on the main path, he engraved additional markings.

Finally, he made his way down the path and chiseled yet more engravings onto the side of the mountain near the main entryway.

Satisfied with his artistry, he made his way down the path to his camel, climbed atop, and departed the area. He first rode through an ancient, sleepy little village. He then made his way down a dusty trail and headed back towards *Medina* and his mistress.

Arabia, after *Hijra,* or 663 AD

The manservant climbed off his camel near the *Temple Mount* in the dead of night. *The Dome of the Rock* would not be built for years to come. He scanned the quiet area and saw no one.

He secured his engraving tools and found the location he was sent to incise. He crawled over the foundation rock and imprinted some etchings onto it.

Satisfied, he inspected his work and mounted his camel. He rode off into the moonlit night.

Chapter Eighteen

The young man who had shot at Burns and al-Hakim in Cambridge deplaned from his Saudi Airlines flight in *Medina*. He checked his phone and found a text:

> *Our contacts in Medina confirm they are at the Hotel International. Kill them and get the necklace.*

He made his way to the curb and hailed a taxicab. The cab whisked him away and headed towards the hotel in the heart of *Medina*, Saudi Arabia.

At the hotel, Burns went up to the room to freshen up while al-Hakim stopped in the lobby, called and booked a flight to Amman leaving in three hours. He secured a rental car there that would take them to *Jerusalem*. He went up to the room and lay down on a bed.

Burns came from the bathroom and said, "You want something from the vending machine?"

"No. Thank you, Patrick."

Burns departed the room and went to the lobby. He stopped and bought a soda from the vending machine. Just as he withdrew his soda, he saw the man from Cambridge enter the lobby. *Damn, this guy gets around!* He watched the man approach the concierge.

He twisted the cap off his soda bottle. From his vantage point, near the stairwell on the far side of the room, the man could not see him. He ducked into the stairwell and ran up to the third floor, burst into his room to find al-Hakim asleep.

"Ahmed, get up."

Al-Hakim awoke abruptly and snorted. "What it is, Patrick?"

Gathering his belongings, Burns said, "The man from Cambridge is in the lobby."

Al-Hakim sat up and stuffed his belongings into his backpack. "Oh my. That was quick. They must have some network of spies."

"Yeah. It appears we're being watched everywhere. Let's go."

Al-Hakim followed Burns down the hallway. They ducked into the stairwell just as the elevator opened up revealing Cambridge man. He rushed down the hall, found their room, shot at the door handle, kicked open the door and burst in. He searched the room but only saw ruffled bedspreads. He scurried to the window and pulled back the drapes. Peering out, he saw al-Hakim and Burns climbing into a taxi. He bolted for the door, ran down the stairwell and into the parking lot.

Al-Salah's henchman Hamed disembarked from his flight in *Medina*. He placed a call. "I am at the airport," he said.

"They are there as well," said the Cambridge man over the phone. "I am pulling up in a taxicab now."

Hamed disconnected the call and started searching for the two professors.

Al-Hakim negotiated with the attendant at the gate and managed to book standby tickets on an earlier flight, already boarding, to Amman.

"Royal Jordanian Airlines flight twenty-two," announced a man over the loud speaker, "with non-stop service to Amman now boarding all rows through gate eleven."

Burns and al-Hakim waited at the entrance to the jet-way. The line of passengers made their way onto the plane. A moment later the attendant approached and handed them boarding passes. "You are clear to board," the attendant said.

Burns followed al-Hakim down the jet-way.

Hamed spotted them entering the jet-way. He hurried over to the gate and argued with the attendant. Getting nowhere, he had to settle for a ticket on the next flight, the one al-Hakim and Burns had originally booked. He searched through his mobile phone for a contact. He found the one he wanted and sent off a text message:

Two men, an American, Burns, and an Egyptian, al-Hakim, are on flight twenty-two from Medina. I will have photos emailed to you shortly. Follow them, keep your distance, and wait for my arrival and instructions.

The man from Cambridge ran up to the gate.

"Get a ticket on the next flight to Amman," Hamed said to him. He then paced throughout the seating area for a while until the next flight finally boarded.

In Amman, a Jordanian man, dressed in a suit with an unbuttoned shirt, no tie, watched as the passengers disembarked from flight twenty-two from *Medina*. He glanced at the two grainy photographs he held in his hand depicting Burns and al-Hakim. He saw them walk off the plane and into the lobby. He followed them to the car rental center where al-Hakim checked out a car. The attendant handed him the keys. They headed to the rental lot where they found their vehicle and drove off.

The Jordanian tailed them in his own sedan from a safe distance, both cars heading towards Israel.

He watched as Israeli border guards inspected the professors' papers. After satisfying the requirements of the Israelis, they were granted entry. They drove off.

The Jordanian sailed through the Israeli checkpoint at the Israel/Jordan border as well. He followed al-Hakim and Burns into East *Jerusalem* where Burns parked at the bus station near Jeremiah's Grotto. He and al-Hakim walked into the Old City through the Damascus gate. The Jordanian followed.

To their left, Burns and al-Hakim passed the *Zedekia* Cave and walked through the Muslim Quarter. King *Zedekia* had used the cave as an escape route to Jericho as he fled the Babylonians. The Muslim Quarter was a bustling bazaar. They passed the intersection of *Via Dolorosa*, the Way of Sorrows, where Christian pilgrims symbolically relived the events of Jesus' passion.

They saw *the Dome of the Rock* ahead. *The Dome of the Rock* was not a mosque, but a shrine for pilgrims, built by the Muslims atop the ruins of King Solomon's Temple, or the *Temple Mount*. The *Temple Mount* was the most sacred place in Judaism. The temple's foundations still stood. This

The Lost *Hadīth*

was where, at the western foundation, Jews prayed today, called the Western Wall or the Wailing Wall. The site has sacred significance to all three major religions. For the Jews, this was where King Solomon, King David's son, built his temple. For the Christians, this was where Jesus impressed the Jewish sages. Muslims believed this was where Muhammad ascended into heaven with the Angel Gabriel on his night journey. For all three, it was the site where Abraham had built an altar to sacrifice his son, Isaac, and where Jacob saw a golden ladder leading up to heaven. The Muslim Dome was originally built between the years 688 and 691 AD by the Umayyad *caliph* Abd al-Malik.

The Jordanian, not far behind, stopped and pretended to be interested in some trinkets at a street vendor. He saw the professors approach the Western Wall and the temporary wooden bridge connecting the Western Wall Plaza to the *Mugrabi* Gate, also known as the Gate of the Moroccans.

Burns, al-Hakim and other Muslim Pilgrims made their way across the grounds of the *Temple Mount*. Orthodox Jews would never set foot on the *Temple Mount* and were forbidden to do so by rabbinical law. They hold that Jews are not permitted to set foot there until the Jewish Messiah comes.

They made their way past the *Dome of Moses* and the *Qaitbay* Well. Burns glanced up at the moon that adorned the dome of the *Dome of the Rock*, aligned so that if one could see through it, it would point straight toward *Mecca*. The dome itself was quite impressive. Both he and al-Hakim had been here many times for their studies, but each time they had to stop and admire the structure and its religious significance.

While waiting in line with the pilgrims who had gathered there, Burns continued to appreciate the building's exterior. The lower half was all white marble. The top half built with multicolored Turkish tiles. The Arabic inscription around the octagonal part of the dome had verses from the *Qur'an*, most notably *sūrah* 17 describing Muhammad's night journey.

At the checkpoint manned by members of the Muslim Council, they followed the other pilgrims and made it inside. The Muslim Council was an Islamic group allowed by Israel to administer and control access to the site.

Inside, Burns admired more of the architecture. The dome itself had been originally gold, but the elements had made it necessary to replace, most recently using aluminum covered in gold leaf donated by the late King of Jordan. The actual rock, where Jewish history says Abraham had offered to sacrifice his son, Isaac, and where Muslims believed Muhammad ascended into heaven on his night journey, was enshrined by an arched wall or octagonal arcade. The outer floor between the exterior wall and the inner area was laid with a green carpet. The area around the open space between this and the inner area around the rock was carpeted in a lush red. Burns stood there in awe at the magnificent design including the marble columns, the elaborate floral decorations in red and gold, and the main inscription commemorating the Arabic leader Saladin who recaptured the area from the Christian Crusaders. Similarly, the multicolored Mosaics and inscriptions from the *Qur'an* that adorned the interior always impressed Burns.

They spent a great deal of time examining the incredible markings on the structure. Al-Hakim fixed his eyes upon the cupola directly above the rock. It featured floral designs and various inscriptions. There seemed to be nothing out of the ordinary there.

Burns examined the small reliquary that contained hairs from Muhammad's beard. The thought flashed through his mind that forensic scientists could examine the DNA and perhaps make some discoveries, even prove which imams today were actually related to him, but that was certainly out of the question!

Burns glanced over at the Jordanian on the other side of the rock. The Jordanian stared back at them. Burns saw the Jordanian quickly avert his eyes away from him. Burns looked away as well and went back to his business, but he now realized the man had been at the airport in Amman and had followed them through the old city. Additionally, many of the pilgrims had come and gone, while this man, like them, lingered about.

"Patrick, I have not seen anything out of the ordinary, and as this structure has been built and re-built since the time of A'isha, it occurred to me, unless she had influence beyond the grave, there would be no clues on the structure. However..." He motioned for Burns to follow him to the other side of the rock. As they moved, Burns saw the Jordanian move as well, but in the opposite direction, keeping his distance behind newly arrived pilgrims.

"Look there." Al-Hakim pointed at the rock five feet from them. "Do you see?"

"Muhammad's imprints from his night journey," Burns said.

"That is what the faithful would say. Now look to the left and slightly down from there near the under-part of the edge. Over there." He pointed again.

"Yes, I see it," Burns said. "It looks like tiny markings, a symbol, and some Arabic writing." He stared at it for a long moment, but could not see the detail. "There's no way we can just climb down there and take a look." Burns furrowed his brow.

Al-Hakim thought a moment. "Why not?"

"What do you mean?"

"I mean we have to climb down there and get a closer look," al-Hakim said. "We came this far."

"Are you crazy, Ahmed? Look around you."

Al-Hakim scanned the crowd, particularly the Muslim Council guards keeping a keen eye on the pilgrims. "Not now. We can come back tonight."

"You're kidding?"

"Look, Patrick, no padlock is placed on the door. They only have two sentries patrolling the grounds to ensure there is no vandalism."

"Did you notice each carries a mean-looking *jambiya*?"

"I did, but we will have to be careful. Let us go get something to eat and come back tonight."

"Okay, but you seem to be getting too much into this cloak and dagger business."

Al-Hakim smiled.

They departed the Dome, none too soon because a council member started to watch them more closely. They had been there unusually long, more so than the average pilgrim.

Burns noticed the Jordanian following them. He figured they

should stay in crowded areas and keep their distance from him. He did not want to alarm al-Hakim, although he realized al-Hakim was now giddy by this clandestine affair.

They made their way back through the Muslim and Jewish Quarters to the Armenian Quarter where they found the popular and always busy Armenian *Taverna* on *Armenian Patriarchate* Road. A charming restaurant, it had a fountain, a large chandelier and soft Armenian music played in the background. They sat at a table near the fountain.

Burns watched the Jordanian across the street pretending to examine tourist clothing on an outdoor rack. It seemed too obvious that a well-dressed man was interested in cheap T-shirts tourists bought to take back to their families, especially ones depicting the Israeli flag.

A waiter came by and gave Burns and al-Hakim menus. "My government's treat," Burns said.

Burns ordered the *Basturma*, dried beef simmered in spices and al-Hakim ordered the *Khaghoghi Derev*, minced meat in grape leaves. They each ordered bottled water. Throughout their meal, Burns kept a close eye on the Jordanian across the street.

Chapter Nineteen

The two men who accosted al-Hakim and Burns on the street near the University of Cambridge made their way through the *Jaffa Gate* of the Old City and strolled down David Street. To their right stood the Church of Christ and their left the Church of John the Baptist. A mobile phone rang and one of the men answered. "Yes. Okay," he said into his phone and closed it. "They are here," he said to the other man. "They were spotted near *al-Aqsa*. We will go there now."

On the opposite side of the Old City, Hamed and his accomplice entered through the Zion Gate. They hurried up the street past the House of Hanna and made their way over to the Armenian Quarter where they met up with the Jordanian near the thrift shop. The Jordanian said, "They are across the street at the *Armenian Taverna*."

"We have it from here." Hamed handed the Jordanian a wad of cash. The Jordanian departed while Hamed and his accomplice watched the professors eat.

Burns noticed the men meeting and the exchange. He recognized the man from Cambridge and from the hotel in *Medina*. He stood up, went to the restroom and surveyed the back of the restaurant.

He returned to the table where he and al-Hakim finished their meal. Burns continued to watch the two men watching them. The sun was setting over West *Jerusalem*. He paid for the meal, leaving a generous tip and said, "Don't react, and I don't want to alarm you, Ahmed, but we are being watched."

Al-Hakim nodded.

"There are two men, across the street at the thrift shop."

"Yes." Al-Hakim dabbed his lips.

"The restroom is in the back. A gate there leads out into an alley. When I say, get up to go, and I'll meet you at *The Monastery of the Flagellation*. I have an idea as to where we can enter the Dome from there. I'm going to throw these clowns off our trail and pick up some supplies. My watch indicates it is eight o'clock."

Al-Hakim set his watch to exactly that time.

"Stay near the entrance to the monastery," Burns said. "There's a bench in front. I'll meet you there at nine o'clock. Go now, my friend."

Al-Hakim stood up and headed towards the restroom in the back of the restaurant. Burns departed the restaurant and headed towards the thrift store.

Hamed saw him coming and darted his eyes around searching for al-Hakim. *Had Burns figured it out? Why was he coming straight at them?* "Go, search for al-Hakim," Hamed said to his accomplice.

The Cambridge man took off and darted across the street, avoiding Burns who fast approached.

Hamed stepped into the shop, getting out of Burns' way. He hovered near women's lotions. Some of the western advertisements using bikini-clad women on the bottles and displays caused him to flush. He watched Burns grab two small flashlights, a can of bug spray, a lighter, and some twine.

Burns went to the back of the shop and found a multi-faceted screwdriver and a small hammer. On the way back to the cashier, he picked up some etching paper in the children's gift section and stuffed it under his arm. He paid the cashier, placed the items in his backpack and walked up the street.

Hamed departed the shop and followed him from a safe distance.

The Cambridge man searched though the restaurant for al-Hakim. However, he found no sign of him. He noticed the gate at the rear of the restaurant and opened it into the alley. He searched up and down the alley, but saw no sign of al-Hakim, so he closed the gate and rejoined Hamed as he followed Burns up the street.

Burns had been to the Old City many times so he knew his way around, probably better than most who lived there. He had actually made his own maps and an overlay of how it might have been at the time of Jesus. He had an illustrator use his maps to make some illustrations for the two books he had written.

He walked at a fast clip. As he rounded a corner, he saw Hamed and his accomplice trotting to catch up. Burns usually ran three miles a day every morning before breakfast, so this brisk walk was a breeze for him.

He passed the *Church of the Holy Redeemer* and saw some sort of candlelight vigil, a procession heading into the *Church of the Holy*

Sepulcher; must be a night mass, he figured, slowing down and stepping into the end of the line. A young boy, perhaps thirteen years old at most, handed him a candle with a wax-catch at the bottom. He passed another young boy who lit his candle.

    Hamed and his co-conspirator caught up, but not before more people joined the procession into the church. Hamed's heart palpitated somewhat as he realized he was entering the holiest site in all of Christianity.
    A young male docent explained to the pilgrims and tourists: "The Church of the Holy Sepulcher was originally built by Constantine's mother in 330 AD. It is where Jesus was believed to have been crucified on the cross, on a hill called *Gol'gotha,* and buried in a tomb where he was resurrected on the third day."
    This made Hamed faintly nervous, a bead of sweat dripped off his brow. He regained his poise, figuring his qualms were ridiculous, because he was actually acting in the cause of his master, and the fact that Islam considered Jesus a prophet.
    He and the Cambridge man followed Burns across the courtyard. They made their way into the structure through the entrance at *Crusader Façade*. Inside, the pilgrims broke up and mingled near the *Stone of Unction*. Hamed watched Burns as he moved on into the rotunda and around the *Chapel of the Angel*. He said to his henchman, "Stay here, survey the area, and make sure no one follows. Make sure he does not slip back out this way. I'll take care of this." He went around to the back of the tomb monument. His accomplice stayed put, scanning the area. Hamed heard some light singing in the distance coming from the *Chapel of Helen* on the other side of the church. No pilgrims were in this area as they were at the service going on in the *Chapel of Helen*. A few candles flickered around the monument from the breeze blowing in from the entrance near where they had entered.
    He searched for Burns, but he was nowhere. *How could this be?* Then, he found a small entrance behind the tomb monument. It led to some

The Lost *Hadīth*

first century tombs. He stepped inside and into an outer chamber. There was still no sign of Burns. He took out his dagger and held it at the ready. He crept along near an open tomb. A dimly lit candle flickered, then extinguished. The chamber went dark. He froze in his tracks. The only sound he heard was his shallow breathing. He waited in this position for more than a minute. *Perhaps Burns hadn't come through this passage. No, he had to have passed through here. There is nowhere else to go.* He figured Burns must have realized he was on to him. He knew, now, he had lost the element of surprise. He could be a reasonable man. He cleared his throat. "I only want the necklace," he said softly in Arabic. "I wish you no harm."

Nothing. Frustrated, he moved forward again. "You can make this easy or make it difficult," Hamed called out. He pursed his lips in frustration, edged forward and rounded a corner near another tomb. Out of nowhere, an object struck him across his face. He tumbled backwards, staggering a little, and dropped his dagger. The rather large stone that had struck him across the face fell nearby. A large figure lunged at him out of a tomb. Burns was on him in a flash, pounding Hamed using closed fists. Hamed tried to block the blows, but Burns had gotten in several. Hamed fell to the floor unconscious.

Burns grabbed Hamed's *jambiya* and stuffed it into the small of his back. He pulled the twine out of his backpack and bound Hamed's hands, then his feet. It would hold him for a while...at least until al-Hakim and he had accomplished their mission.

Hamed began to stir, so Burns used the *jambiya* to tear off a portion of Hamed's expensive Armani sports jacket. He stuffed it into Hamed's mouth and tied some twine around Hamed's head to hold the rag in place. He grabbed his backpack and headed through the opening in the wall.

He stopped cold upon seeing Hamed's co-conspirator standing near the *Coptic Chapel,* his back to him. He heard, then saw, some pilgrims approaching from the other side of the *edicule*. The man was distracted by the approaching pilgrims, so Burns capitalized on the distraction and slipped out the other side of the Chapel.

He made his way through the *Armenian Shrine*, passed the *Stone of Unction*, and out the *Crusaders entrance*. Outside, he dropped the *jambiya* into a trash receptacle. He hung a quick left and walked at a fast pace making his way over to *Via Dolorosa*.

He rendezvoused with al-Hakim at the *Monastery of the Flagellation* and sat on the bench next to him. "I figure we can go through the *Bab-el-Atim*," he said.

"That is usually not an entrance that is used," al-Hakim said. "How will we get through?"

"With this." Burns showed him the screwdriver from his backpack. Al-Hakim didn't question him. They waited until the pedestrian traffic died down. Burns picked up a rock that fit into the palm of his hand and dropped it into his pack.

The *Bab-el-Atim* was the *Gate of Darkness*, the first entrance along the Northern wall of the *Temple Mount*; what the Muslims called the *al-Aqsa* Sanctuary.

"Let's go," Burns said a few minutes later. Al-Hakim jumped up and followed him as they made their way down *Sha'ar Ha-Arayot* in the direction of Lion's Gate.

They took a right turn a short distance later onto *Ha-Melekh Faisal* and made their way over to *Bab-el-Atim*. Two people walked past them near the gate. "Keep watch, while I get us in," said Burns.

Al-Hakim stood guard, his back to Burns who approached the gate. He worked on the gate for a time, managing to unscrew two hinges and a latch. He used the hammer and lightly tapped the latch open. He pried the gate back, just enough for a human to squeeze through. "Ahmed," he whispered, then slid through the opening.

Al-Hakim followed him through the opening and closed the gate behind him. They made their way over to the *Dome of the Spirits* and took cover. A sentry sat on a chair near the *Bab ed Jenneh*, the *Door to Paradise*.

Not far away, near the *Dome of the Chain*, Burns saw the two men who had accosted them in Cambridge hiding there on the other side. He whispered to al-Hakim, "They're all over the place." He threw the rock from his backpack. It landed on the far side of the *Prayer Niche of the Prophet*. The sentry heard it and moved around the dome building to investigate. As soon as he did, Burns and al-Hakim slipped into the *Dome of The Rock* through the *Bab ed Jenneh*.

The Lost *Ḥadīth*

Inside the Dome, Burns hurried to the markings they saw earlier, al-Hakim following. They climbed down onto the sacred rock. Fortunately, the markings were not on the main part of the rock, so many would not find it too much of a desecration. Burns was vigilant not to step on Muhammad's footprints; however, he was tempted to size them up.

He handed al-Hakim one of the flashlights. Al-Hakim steadied it on the markings while Burns pulled the etching paper out of his backpack. He rubbed the etching paper, leaving the imprints of the markings on it. After he finished, he examined what he had. Satisfied, he folded it and placed it in his pack.

Next, he took out a digital camera and snapped several photographs of the markings. He readjusted the camera's settings and took several close-ups. He checked the pictures he had taken, and satisfied, he put the camera back in his pack.

He closely examined the markings using the loupe. There it was again, the woman on the back of the camel, yet this one had two directional arrows, one pointing east, halfway between three and four o'clock, and the other pointing not directly south, but halfway between five and six o'clock.

He stood over the directional symbols and used his compass to note the first directional symbol, the east one, between three and four o'clock, and found an azimuth that read ninety-two degrees. The second directional pointer, the south one, between five and six o'clock, had an azimuth of one hundred fifty-seven degrees. He recorded both azimuths in his notebook.

Outside the Dome, the sentry walked around to the other side near the *Bab el Qibleh,* the *South Door*. He circled around and came upon the *Dome of the Chain*. One of the two Cambridge men walked up to the sentry while the other crouched down on the other side of the *Dome of the Chain*.

The one man approaching the sentry said, "Good evening, my brother."

The sentry said, "Stop. You are not allowed here at this time of the night."

"I was just here to see the Dome." He motioned with his hand causing the sentry to turn his head to follow the man's movements.

The other man came up from behind the sentry, spun him around and punched him in the face. The sentry fell to the ground.

The men dragged the sentry behind the *Dome of the Chain*.

Burns and al-Hakim departed *the Dome of The Rock* through the *Bab ed Jenneh*. Another sentry appeared from the opposite direction near the *Prayer Niche of the Prophet* and stopped in his tracks upon seeing them.

"Let's go," Burns said to al-Hakim. They jogged in the opposite direction towards the *Dome of the Chain* and came upon the scene there; the two Cambridge men and the unconscious sentry.

The conscious sentry near the *Prayer Niche of the Prophet* ran after them yelling, "Stop there!"

Everyone stopped. The two Cambridge men dropped the unconscious sentry and confronted the professors.

Burns un-slung his backpack, reached in, and pulled out the bug spray and lighter. He sprayed the can and lit the flume. It shot out and startled the two Cambridge men, singeing their hair and eyebrows. As they reacted to their predicament, bringing their hands up to their burnt faces, Burns rushed them, gut punching one. The man fell to the ground clutching his abdomen. Burns flung around and kicked the other in the chest knocking him to the ground.

The conscious sentry said into his hand-held radio, his voice elevated, "I need assistance. There are men here."

Burns turned around, faced the conscious sentry, and said in Arabic, "These men are trying to desecrate our holy *al-Aqsa*."

The conscious sentry seemed confused, squinting at Burns.

"You subdue them and we'll go get help." Burns picked up his backpack and stuffed the bug spray into it.

The conscious sentry nodded.

Burns, taking advantage of the pain and disorientation the two men Cambridge men were in, as well as the confusion the conscious sentry seemed to be in, grabbed al-Hakim by his arm and led him off, running towards the *Bab el-Atim*. There, they slipped out through the gate. Al-Hakim stood guard while Burns worked on re-attaching the gate latch and hinges.

The Cambridge men back at the *Dome of the Chain* regained their bearings. They attacked the conscious sentry, hitting him in the face. The frightened conscious sentry fell to the ground, bleeding from his nose.

    The two Cambridge men staggered in the direction Burns and al-Hakim had fled. Their eyebrows singed and eyelids sore, they tried to refocus.

    Burns finished re-attaching the hinges and the latch just as the Cambridge men arrived on the other side and banged on the door.

    "Let's go," Burns said, leading al-Hakim along the *Sha'ar Ha-Arayot* to *Via Dolorosa* where they turned right onto *Ha-Gai* Street towards the *Damascus Gate* of the Old City. They jogged to their rental car and headed out for the airport in Amman, Jordan.

Chapter Twenty

She departed the Howard-Tilton Memorial Library and headed over to the St. Charles Streetcar stop near Tulane University in New Orleans. Sara worked part-time in the campus library. The streetcar went all the way down St. Charles Street past Tulane and Loyola Universities and Audubon Park. This provided a convenient mode of transportation for the students who needed to get to their boarding houses in the Garden District as well as down to Canal Street and to the French Quarter.

The semester over several weeks ago and summer in full swing, she had finished her first year of graduate school. Her course of study centered on a Masters in Public Health and International Health and Development.

She looked forward to her Paris trip which her father had been generous to help pay. She had received his text and after she bordered the streetcar, sat down and sent him one:

Dad. On my way to Paris tomorrow. Love, Sara.

Burns' daughter was a slender and stunning young woman with warm, captivating brown eyes. She had a dark olive complexion and her skin was smooth as silk. The breeze from the open streetcar window fluttered her long, black and shiny hair across her face. She could pass for an Arabian princess and closely resembled her mother, Fatima.

A young man boarded the streetcar after Sara and sat five seats behind her. He was of Iraqi decent, well-groomed and dressed casual American style in a blue Polo shirt, tan slacks and loafers. He wore dark sunglasses to hide his staring eyes. However, this was not out of the ordinary, as many foreign students attended American universities.

He watched Sara as she got off at Second Street. He followed her and other passengers and departed the streetcar, most splitting off in several directions. He kept his distance, followed her down to Prytania Street, two other students meandering in front of him. He studied her, admiring her beauty. In another time, in another world perhaps, he would have asked her father for her hand in marriage.

He watched her enter a large, extravagant Queen Ann style house with two gables adorning it. He continued down the sidewalk past the house and stood on the corner of Second and Coliseum. He tapped out a text on his phone:

I have located the Burns girl.

He sent the message off, pocketed the phone and walked back up to Prytania Street where he hovered near the house.

Inside the house, Sara packed for her Paris trip. She lovingly remembered the time she and her parents vacationed there. They had such a wonderful time. She admired the way her parents got along together and how deeply in love they were. Someday she hoped she would fall in love the way they had. She wiped away a tear that ran down her cheek. She wished her mother could have lived to see her receive her bachelor's degree and follow her on through graduate school. She struggled to put these memories out of her mind so she could concentrate on packing.

The Lost *Hadīth*

Colonel Graves shuffled down a hallway in the new and elaborate American embassy in Baghdad. The embassy was now the largest, most extensive and expensive one of its kind in the world. In fact, the embassy was completely self-sufficient; it had its own electrical generating capabilities, water, and its own area code. The American government built it to be a small city within a city capable of running itself requiring no dependence on Baghdad or Iraqi services. Many governmental agencies had begun to move in to their respective offices.

Graves, who doubled as an officer working for the Central Intelligence Agency's Special Activities Division, was in charge of an American black-ops unit that trained Iraqi military and special operations services.

He entered his office and sifted through the mail piled atop his desk. A young and attractive female entered.

"Colonel?"

"Yes, Captain?"

"More on Major Eugene Cunningham's disappearance." She handed him a paper.

He sat in his chair and scanned the document.

The captain waited for him to finish. "Major Garrett is on his way," she said.

"Okay." He sighed. "Send him in when he arrives." She turned and left the office.

Graves set the document on his desk and fingered through the rest of his mail.

A few minutes later, Major Garrett arrived. In his early thirties, tall and rugged, he held his beret in his right hand and a briefcase in his left.

"What've you got?" Graves said. He motioned for Garrett to sit in the chair opposite him.

"Our sources confirm Cunningham is being held by Hasan Ali al-Salah," Garrett said.

"Damn. That fucker again?" Graves leaned back.

"Our sources also inform us Cunningham is being held in Sadr City in an area controlled by al-Salah. We have actionable intelligence it could be one of three particular storefronts owned by an al-Salah accomplice."

Graves leaned in close to Garrett. "Find him and get him the hell outta there, but I want the Iraqis to lead on this. Al-Salah has control over that section of the city. This has to be an Iraqi operation. We need cover."

"Understood, Colonel. I'll get right on it." Garrett departed the office.

Graves sat there stewing that if it hadn't been for that asshole, al-Salah, Americans could have been out of Iraq in large part two to three years earlier than projected. Al-Salah could have had his domain, but his perpetuation of the civil strife kept him from obtaining that which we wanted as a result anyway. Made no sense whatsoever. If only he, Graves, had the authority, he would have had this bastard killed years ago.

Graves worked his phone the rest of the day trying to get information on Burns and his progress and a host of other issues concerning joint American/Iraqi counter terrorist operations in progress or development.

Chapter Twenty-One

They made their way back to the airport in Amman and caught a flight to Cairo. There, they hailed a taxicab and headed for a residence near Cairo University in Giza, Egypt.

Ascending the stairs to the modest apartment, al-Hakim's wife came out to greet them. She was in her middle fifties, dressed in western attire, slacks and a blouse. She had short black hair and was petite in stature. She held open the door to the apartment to let the two men pass.

Inside, al-Hakim gave her a kiss and a hug. She then turned to Burns who kissed her on her cheek. He hugged her as well. "Johara," Burns said. "So good to see you again."

"And you, Patrick. Please." She waived her arm for him to make himself at home. "Let us eat. I have prepared a meal."

The two men dropped their packs near the door. Burns set his satchel on the living room table. The apartment was simple, small, yet had two bedrooms and one bathroom. It was simply decorated in Egyptian décor. Burns and al-Hakim sat at the dining room table. The dining room and living room were one and the same.

Johara served them a traditional Egyptian meal consisting of Egyptian potato, onion lamb casserole. For dessert, they ate an Egyptian cake, cream butter and sugar with a touch of chocolate topped with chopped walnuts.

After the meal, they relaxed on the balcony that faced the great pyramids of Giza. They drank *Karkady*, a Hibiscus tea made from the dried, dark red petals of the Hibiscus flower. Johara sweetened their drinks with standard sugar.

Burns turned on his phone and checked messages. There was nothing from Cunningham, so he shot him a text:

Had a couple incidents with different assailants trying to steal the necklace. Review the security process for this operation and see if you can plug the leaks. We really need you to stop this interference so we can go about finding this ḥadīth. We are making progress but these narrow escapes are getting narrower. Let me know what you find out. Burns.

Next, he read the text from Sara. He, too, thought about their trip to Paris years earlier. He saw Fatima and Sara walking next to him along the River Seine. A deep and profound sense of emptiness filled his heart. He replied:

Have fun. Love, Dad.

After their tea, the two men went back into the living room. Johara relaxed on the balcony and read a book. Burns pulled his notes from his satchel. He spread out the old maps, illustrations and the etching he had made at the Dome.

Al-Hakim downloaded the photos from the camera onto his computer and printed them out. He spread them out on the table next to the etching and maps. "Look at this," Burns said, pointing to one of the photographs. He said, in Arabic:

بكر انتقل الى رحمة الله تعالى لكن كان الصفه
اظهرت طريقة على سلك - ولكها

Then said it in English, "Bakr went to the mercy of Allah, yet the *Suffah* hath showed, a path for one to follow." He transcribed it in his notebook.

"Yes," al-Hakim said. "A slight variation on the one we found at *Al-Masjid al-Nabawi.*" He studied a photograph of the woman on the back of the camel.

Burns looked up at him and said, "It seems to indicate we may have correctly followed the clues the pendant left and are on the right path."

"Perhaps," al-Hakim said. "However, if one had only found this clue in this context, one would have no idea what this meant. It would seem

The Lost Hadīth

to be nothing more than gibberish."

"Right," Burns said. "Without the pendant, which is clearly needed to begin this journey, none of this would make any sense." He studied the etchings he made at the Dome.

"The pendant led us first to the *Al-Masjid al-Nabawi*, which then pointed us in the direction of the Dome," Al-Hakim said, scanning his notes and thinking aloud. "But does the path continue on towards *Basra*?"

"I think it does," Burns said. "A'isha perpetrated this, using her scribes or servants to carry this out, so she is clearly pointing us next in the direction of The Battle of the Camel near *Basra*." He studied the etching depicting the woman on the back of a camel, the directional arrows next to it.

"Because," al-Hakim said, "the battle is an integral historical occurrence in the history of Islam and therefore must also be an integral clue in this quest, especially because it was an important event in A'isha's life. She clearly incorporated this event, her event, into this pursuit." Al-Hakim studied the etching again. "So, again, on this etching from *the Dome of the Rock*," he said, "there are two directional symbols."

"Yes," Burns said, jotting down notes in his journal. He oriented the directional arrows on a map of the area based on the pictures, etchings and azimuths they had recorded. "I have an idea," Burns said, rearranging the picture of the woman on the back of the camel, the one having the two directional arrows. "Could you give me a ruler, Ahmed?"

Al-Hakim opened a desk drawer nearby, took out a ruler, and handed it to him.

Using the first azimuth setting, the south one between five and six o'clock, Burns drew a line using a marker out from *Jerusalem* extending it all the way out onto the regional map. The line went straight down to *Mecca*. He then drew another line, using the second azimuth he had recorded from the compass heading at *the Dome of the Rock*, between three and four o'clock, and drew a line that went from *Jerusalem* straight to *Basra*.

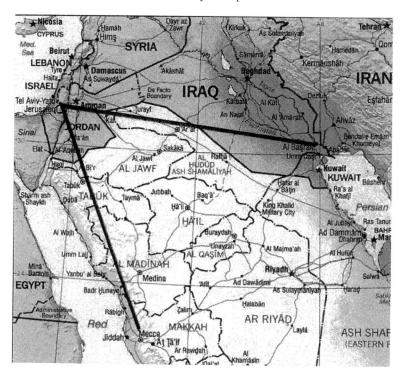

"Look at that," Burns said.

"Three points that form a large V." Al-Hakim studied the map.

"They're three important and critical cities in the history of Islam," Burns noted. "But what else could this V mean?"

Al-Hakim tapped his finger on the map. "But here," he said, pointing to an ancient map of the *Basra* area, "is the *Wadi-us-Saba*."

"The Valley of the Lion, where The Battle of the Camel was fought," Burns said, thinking aloud.

"Okay. Let us think," al-Hakim said, studying the regional map that included the *Wadi-us-Saba*. "The clues at *Al-Masjid al-Nabawi* pointed us to *Jerusalem* which we inferred was actually *the Dome of the Rock*. At *Jannat al-Baqi* the clues pointed to *Basra*." He took out the other map Burns had drawn the line on from *Medina* to *Basra*. He ran his finger along on the map of the region tracing the V Burns had just drawn. "From *Medina* to *Jerusalem*," al-Hakim continued, "but back to *Mecca* from *Jerusalem* we have been directed. Then from *Jerusalem* to *Basra* which gives us this V. From *Medina* to *Basra*, but from *Basra* back to, where?"

"Back to *Medina* or *Mecca*?" Burns scratched his nose.

"It could point us to either one." Al-Hakim scrutinized the etching again. "But I would think we have already found all there is to find in *Medina*."

"I agree," Burns said. "She would not just direct us back where we started."

"So, as we infer from these clues, I would say there must be something near *Wadi-us-Saba* that points us back to *Mecca* or somewhere else." Al-Hakim thought for a long time. "Even though the line on this map with the azimuths you have configured goes straight to *Basra*, the line on this other map does not go directly through *Basra* but does go near where we believe the *Wadi-us-Saba* may have been. I think that is where we should look."

"I agree," Burns said, tapping his pencil on the map with the V, "as that is where the battle occurred. However, where would we even begin to look in that area? You know how vast it is." Burns considered the ancient map of the region near *Wadi-us-Saba*.

"I do not know. However, we could reconnoiter in that region near *Khuraiba*. We can start in *Basra* and work our way out."

"We could."

"What have we got to lose?" al-Hakim said.

"Absolutely nothing." Burns folded the map and put it in his satchel.

"This is a lot of fun, do you not think, Patrick?"

"Well, not with assassins chasing you." Burns closed his notebook.

Al-Hakim grunted. "Yes, well, we should get a fresh start in the morning." He folded the etching and handed it to Burns who packed it in his satchel. "We should go to *al-Azhar* tomorrow morning," al-Hakim said. "It has the best available artifacts in the entire world on the subject of The Battle of the Camel."

"Good idea."

They finished packing their research and turned in for the night. Burns slept soundly in the guest room.

Chapter Twenty-Two

Al-Salah sat on a sofa with his feet up on a stool in the living room of his palatial estate. Opulent Arabic decorations adorned the house and several servants worked on cleaning, cooking and attending to his garden outside. A manservant fanned al-Salah using a large palm frond. Another manservant brought him a glass of *Arak*, an Iraqi unsweetened aniseed-flavored alcoholic drink. The manservant placed the glass of *Arak* on an end table next to al-Salah and bowed to him while backing up. Al-Salah picked the glass up to take a sip.

The man who had tortured Cunningham walked into the room and over to al-Salah. "Master," the torturer said. "I have received a message on the major's phone from Professor Burns."

Al-Salah set his drink down on the table next to him and said, "Yes?"

"He has complained about attacks upon him and asked for intervention. They are aware we have spies in their operations. He said he and al-Hakim are progressing in their mission. He seemed to indicate there were others besides us seeking the necklace."

Al-Salah groaned. "Yassim and the brotherhood." He thought for a long moment, leaving his loyal employee waiting for instructions. Finally, he said, "Well, then, I want the other arrangement initiated as we discussed. It seems this Burns is more skillful in certain matters than we expected. In addition, we may need an arrangement with the Brotherhood. Also, move the major. I received information the Americans may have figured out where it is we are holding him."

"Yes, Master." He bowed and departed.

He took another sip of his *Arak* and stared out at his well-manicured botanical garden.

The young Arabic man who had followed Sara in New Orleans sat in a seat several rows behind her on her flight to Paris. He watched her as she slept for most of the flight.

He followed her off the plane upon arrival in Paris in the early morning hours. He followed her as she retrieved her small suitcase from the luggage carousel and made her way to the airport shuttle service. She boarded a bus and found a seat near the front.

The young man boarded the bus as well. He sat several rows behind Sara who had her head bowed over at a street map of Paris.

On the Left Bank of the River Seine, the man followed Sara off the bus and watched as she checked into the *Hotel Degres de Notre-Dame* across the river from the Notre Dame Cathedral. It was a quaint little bed and breakfast hotel with small rooms upstairs and various views, including some of Notre Dame Cathedral.

The man stood hovering and watching the hotel near the wall next to the River Seine. He entered a text into his phone.

An elite, newly trained counterinsurgency unit of the Iraqi military swooped into a confined alleyway off a marketplace in the *Shiite* enclave of Sadr City. They secured the area as a smaller contingent burst through the backdoor of an electronics store. They covered one another as three soldiers broke through a basement door and into a small, dimly lit room, the same room where Cunningham had been tortured. There was a broken chair in the middle of the room and a light bulb dangling above it. The room, unoccupied, had dried blood and teeth all over the floor.

An American military medical technician stepped into the room, put on medical gloves, and pulled out of his pack some Buccal T-Swabs in their accompanying collection tubes. He proceeded to take blood samples off the floor. After taking several samples from different areas of the room and chair, he enclosed each swab by pulling them into the accompanying collection tube and closed the plastic cap. He picked up the teeth and placed them in separate baggies. He scanned the room for more forensic samples, but finding none said, "Let's go." He departed the room, followed by the squad of Iraqi soldiers.

Burns awoke in the early morning hours excited by the task before them. *This whole adventure could be a waste of time, or a wild goose chase,* he thought. However, because he did not have to pay for it, and the fact he was rediscovering important historical events of this fascinating history, perhaps new discoveries, so be it.

He and al-Hakim made their way to the *al-Azhar Mosque* and University. The mosque was founded in 971 AD and the school of theology was founded in 988 AD. The mosque and university was founded in honor of Muhammad's daughter, Fatima Az-Zahraa, the shining one. The structure was decorated with typical Arabian and Egyptian architectural features in the heart of Cairo.

Upon entering, he thought of his own Fatima. He sighed and followed al-Hakim into an ornate reading room where they located several early reproductions of maps of the region, including *Basra*, and some accompanying reference guides. They studied similar versions of the history of The Battle of the Camel and its location. They copied the maps on a copier in the library and made notations of geographical points as to exactly where this event occurred, or might have occurred. Most of these maps were not completely accurate given the time they had been made and the fact the map-making abilities of those at the time were not scientifically correct.

"Okay," al-Hakim said. "So we have The Battle of the Camel in *Wadi-us-Saba*, near here," he pointed on his map, "near the village of *Khuraiba* outside *Basra*. I pinpoint the battle somewhere in this vast area here." He ran his finger along a ridgeline and made a circle of a large area.

"Yes," Burns said, examining the map closely. "It's still quite a vast area and this other map here, shows the area the battle took place in a slightly different area."

Al-Hakim scrutinized the map Burns referenced. "We would have a large area to scour," he said, "and I understand your point of view that there really is nothing there save sand and rocks, perhaps some escarpments."

They compared the two maps to a third map they found. This map, they learned, was a reproduction of a map made by a scribe of Ali at the time of the battle. Although it was crudely drawn, it did have a reference point to *Basra* and *Khuraiba*.

"If this one is accurate," al-Hakim said, "then it narrows the battle area down to within five square kilometers. It may be the most accurate of all the maps because these other two were made much later after the battle from oral accounts."

They analyzed the three maps again.

"So," Burns said, thinking aloud. "We know after the battle Ali had A'isha sent to *Medina*, sort of under house arrest for the rest of her life. This could be about the time she dreamt up this scheme as her chosen successors had now lost control of the ministry, even though she had been told earlier by her father to discard this *ḥadīth*."

"Yes, she clearly held onto this *ḥadīth* until after her disgrace in battle." Al-Hakim rubbed his beard and said, "We agree she may have hid this *ḥadīth* after the Battle of the Camel, perhaps to hold sway over Ali's emerging *Shiites*."

"Maybe," Burns said. "But you don't think she orchestrated this to undermine her father, who had excluded it?"

"I do not think so. She was in agreement with her father on the subject of how the ministry was progressing."

"But not in agreement with his decision to exclude this."

"Although she held onto it until after the battle with Ali," al-Hakim reaffirmed.

"Yes. We may never know for sure her reasons for doing this." Burns considered the etching of the woman on the back of the camel again. He tapped his pencil on the map of the region next to the etching.

"As we know, Patrick, there has been considerable debate amongst scholars for centuries, actually since the time of Muhammad's death, of what is true and what is embellished as to the *aḥādīth*."

"Yes, and scholars authenticated the *aḥādīth* attributed to her." Burns laid his pencil down in the crease of his notebook and massaged his forehead.

"These additional accountings were perhaps not included by her father," al-Hakim started...

"...because he had essentially controlled much of the inclusion in the beginning," Burns continued, "perhaps exclusion of these accountings, then something was clearly excluded because it may have been damaging to the faith."

"And not so much to Ali. But only because after the battle and her disgrace did she orchestrate all of this," al-Hakim said.

"I don't know, Ahmed." Burns sat thinking where all this could lead. He considered the true ramifications of finding this *ḥādīth*. If it indeed had passages damaging to the faith, it could cause a crisis, bloodshed, war, if anyone believed it at all. If it only had passages damaging to Ali, it still would cause strife, albeit sectarian. He stared for a long time at the maps, the illustrations, and the open books on the table in front of them.

"Well," al-Hakim said, snapping out of his own deep thoughts, "let us get back to the task at hand." He turned a page in a book he had been skimming. "If we take this area here," he said, pointing to the detailed map originally drawn by one of Ali's scribes, "we know the battle here was within several kilometers of where our lines intersect. We agree that this is not completely accurate. Nowhere can we find evidence as to the exact location of the house where A'isha was taken, so the clues we seek must be somewhere in the *Wadi-us-Saba*."

Burns nodded and checked a photograph he had taken of the depiction of the woman on the back of the camel at *the Dome of the Rock*. "The *Wadi-us-Saba*."

"I am afraid we will just have to go there and drive around," al-Hakim said. "There must be something there. The clues we have found so far all point us in that direction. The clues from the depictions at the *Jannat al-Baqi* point us to *Basra*, or the *Wadi-us-Saba*. The clues at the *Dome of the Rock* point us to the *Wadi-us-Saba*." Al-Hakim closed the book. "Let us go back to the house and get ready, Patrick. I will make the travel arrangements for *Basra*."

Burns folded the copies of the maps they had made, the etchings, and gathered up the photographs. He packed everything in his satchel. They went back to al-Hakim's house where he and al-Hakim bid farewell to Johara. They were on a flight to Kuwait City a few hours later.

Chapter Twenty-Three

Graves was unpacking files from boxes in his office at the embassy when Major Garrett entered. "Forensics confirmed the blood samples belong to Cunningham," Garrett said.

"Damn." Graves slammed a box onto the floor. "No remains yet?"

"Nothing."

Graves sat and leaned back in his chair, interlocking his hands behind his bald head.

"I have my team searching," Garrett said. "The Iraqis are going house to house, but you know how Sadr City is."

"Fuckin' animals," Graves said. "We need to step this up. Make sure you monitor Burns. We can't afford to have these assholes get hold of these writings, or Burns." He unfolded his hands and leaned forward. "Okay, keep me posted."

Garrett departed the office. Graves picked up his phone and punched in some numbers. "This is Colonel Graves. Is Colonel Mack in? When do you expect him? I need to see him as soon as he can get over here." He hung up the phone.

Sara ate her breakfast at the sidewalk café outside her hotel. She studied a travel guide next to her coffee cup. She circled a few sites she wanted to see, took a bite of her croissant and sipped her coffee. She tapped out a text to her father:

Dad, here in Paris. Everything fine. Planning some sightseeing to museums with Jennifer. Start at the Rodin Museum, then hit the d'Orsay. Love, Sara.

A minute later, Jennifer announced herself as she approached Sara's table. "*Bienvenue à Paris*," she said, throwing open her arms.

Sara stood and gave her a hug. Jennifer sat and adjusted her short skirt and flashy orange blouse. She was a student at the American University of Paris, in her early twenties, and had dark brown roots at the base of her bleached blond hair. Sara poured her some coffee.

"How's your dad?" Jennifer said, dumping creamer in her coffee.

"He's fine."

Jennifer stirred her coffee. "Why doesn't he give that up?"

Sara shrugged. "I think he does it to keep himself busy. He has done nothing but totally immerse himself in his work and the service with the Guard since, well, you know." She stared at her coffee.

Jennifer pressed on, taking a sip of her coffee. "Did they ever find, well, you know, who killed her?"

"No." Sara twirled the coffee in her cup.

"I mean, they never found a motive or anything? Why would someone just randomly kill her like that? It makes no sense to me at all."

Sara said nothing but stared at her coffee.

"I remember how so much in love they were with each other."

Sara squinted at her.

Silence.

Jennifer buttered a croissant and took a bite while watching Sara stare at her coffee. Jennifer said, "Well, it's nice to see you here in *La Ville-Lumière*."

Sara crinkled her map. "Yes, it is. Shall we go to the Rodin first?"

"Oh, that would be great," Jennifer said, taking a sip of her coffee.

The young man who had followed Sara from New Orleans sat a few tables away watching the two girls. He punched a text message into his phone.

Cunningham lay crumpled in the fetal position on a soiled mat on the floor of a darkened concrete room. The room had no light, yet the sun bled through the towel draped in front of a small window on one side of the room. His bloodied face swollen, he rolled over in agony as the door swung open. The brutal torturer who had beaten him earlier entered followed by al-Salah. "Major, you are not making this go well for you. I told you we are a peaceful people."

"You humor me?" Cunningham said through his bloodied lips. "There is nothing I can do for you."

"I will give you one more opportunity to tell me all you know."

"Listen, I told you all I know." Cunningham rolled over and sat up against the back wall, grasping his abdomen and wincing in pain. "Allah will not look kindly upon you."

"I am tiring of your ignorance as to the one true religion." Al-Salah circled back towards the door. "You have forced me to take additional, more extreme measures," he continued, stopping at the door. He turned and faced him. "We will soon have leverage over your Professor, or is it Sergeant Burns?" He cracked a wicked smile. "He'll soon be in a position where he will do what it is we want."

"You're mistaken. Burns can't be bought or blackmailed."

"Oh, but I have found his weakness." Al-Salah paused and studied Cunningham sitting on the floor, his back to the wall. "I will give you one more chance, Major."

Cunningham did not answer.

"Very well. I am not going to kill you. As I have said, we are peaceful and compassionate people."

Cunningham glared up at him again. "You call this compassionate? Look at me."

Al-Salah smiled again. "You Americans are so self-righteous. And so funny. I love American movies. Especially that Mel Brooks. He is such a funny man."

"Yeah, that he is. Really funny."

Al-Salah frowned. "Okay, Major." He turned to go. "You have chosen the wrong path."

"And you. See you in hell, imam."

He stopped, paused, then left the room followed by his torturer.

Outside the door, al-Salah said to his henchman. "Increase surveillance inside the American operation. I want to stay one-step ahead of the Americans. We may have to move the major again. And, go ahead with the Burns girl."

His torturer nodded, climbed into a sedan and sped away. Al-Salah climbed into his own guarded SUV. It drove off down the dusty Sadr City street.

Chapter Twenty-Four

Burns and al-Hakim's flight touched down in Kuwait City. They made their way over to the car rental counter, checked out a Range Rover and drove north towards Iraq.

The Iraqi border guards checked them through. Everything appeared in order so they were allowed to pass. Only recently had the Iraqi government taken control of the southern area, including *Basra* from the British who had withdrawn.

They drove on to *Basra* near where they believed the Battle of the Camel occurred. The *Wadi-us-Saba* was mostly barren desert area near *Basra*. As suspected, there was nothing to indicate exactly where the battle had been, and considering it was waged on December 4, 656 AD, any evidence was certainly long gone.

They drove around the area, backtracking several times on this road, then driving up and down on that road. They spent the entire first day covering many square miles. They marked on a map where they had been and tried to cover as much ground as they could. They stopped many times to examine rocks, escarpments, and small hills, finding nothing.

Frustrated, they drove back into *Basra* and checked into a hotel to rest for the night. Exhausted, they fell asleep right away.

The next morning they paid their bill, ate breakfast at a nearby café, and hit the road. They once again scoured the area and covered new ground, yet found nothing.

"This is not going to help us, Patrick," al-Hakim said, exhausted and frustrated, holding a map in his lap while Burns drove.

Burns stopped the Rover and shifted the gear into park. Al-Hakim consulted his map. "Let us head back towards *Basra*," al-Hakim said, circling his finger on the map of the area near *Basra*. "I think we should ask some questions, perhaps at the local mosque, find the local imam. Maybe someone would know something."

Burns shifted the Rover into gear and headed back to *Basra*. They pulled into town and found a mosque near the heart of the city. Burns stayed in the Rover while al-Hakim went inside. The Rover made an easy target for someone to steal.

Al-Hakim intercepted the imam near his office at the end of a hallway. A young aide hovered nearby looking out the window at Burns in the Rover.

"I am Ahmed al-Hakim. I used to teach at the university in Baghdad. I am studying The Battle of the Camel and wondered if you had a more precise idea as to exactly where the battle had occurred, and as to where the house might have been where A'isha was taken to after her camel had been killed."

The imam, an older man, narrowed his eyes at al-Hakim.

Al-Hakim unfolded the copy of the map Ali's scribe had made. He circled with his finger the area he believed the battle had taken place. "Was it in this area here?"

The imam raised an eyebrow upon seeing such an ancient map and al-Hakim's enthusiasm to find this location. The imam shook his head. "I am sorry. I cannot help you for I know not where the battle took place."

He turned and walked away from al-Hakim who stood there dumbfounded. Al-Hakim knew all too well outsiders were not looked upon or treated favorably, however this was most impolite. He folded the map and returned to Burns in the Rover. "Very distrustful and no help at all," he said.

"Let's go back where we left off and continue our search," Burns said. "I don't think the locals will be any help in this."

Inside the mosque, the young man whispered something in the imam's ear. The imam nodded and said, "I heard a rumor there could be foreigners seeking to desecrate our holy sites. I will notify our brothers."

A mile down the road, al-Hakim, skimming through a biography he had brought along on A'isha, read aloud a quote Ali had said of her after the Battle:

> *Respect must be shown to her because she is the spouse of the Holy Prophet...*

"And to her he said," al-Hakim said continuing, reading from the book:

> *It befits your dignity to remain in your house and not to meddle in politics or to share the rough life of the battlefield, nor to join any party in the future which may tarnish the glory of your name, or become the authoress of a second rebellion.*

Al-Hakim thought a moment.

"What is it, Ahmed?"

"Well, Ali sent her back to *Medina* and placed her under house arrest for the remainder of her life."

"And the *Sunnis* would forever challenge the emerging *Shiite* offshoot for centuries," Burns said, turning off one road and down another, heading back towards the *Wadi-us-Saba*.

"I say there was still bitterness despite what Ali had said," said

al-Hakim. He again read from the book, this time a quote from A'isha:
> *There existed no enmity between Ali and me, save a few petty domestic squabbles.*

"A few petty domestic squabbles? Indeed. I say she kept this going, in part, to hold sway over Ali's followers and descendants if not to challenge their right to rule over the faith. Ali had given her a huge staff, including some forty handmaidens, scribes, and other house servants to care for her until her death in 678 at the age of sixty-six. Her motive in all of this must have been to continue to challenge Ali."

"Although these servants most likely were picked by Ali, out of loyalty to him," Burns said, "perhaps to keep an eye on her as well."

"Yes, but I am sure some switched their loyalty to her after her infectious personality and crisp intelligence weighed upon them. Clearly, she had the word put out that this necklace and pendant existed. Imams have been running around for centuries looking for it."

Burns pulled the Rover over near a roadside stand. A young man, his wife and two children, both boys, worked there. They sold bottled soda, dried fruits and salty snacks. "Let's take a break," Burns said.

They climbed out of the Rover, purchased some dried fruits, and bottled sodas, albeit on the warm side. The man and his wife held back from Burns, so he kept his distance to put them at ease.

Al-Hakim tried to engage the father in a conversation. "I was a professor of Islamic and Arabic studies from Baghdad University."

The father peered at him but did not respond.

"My friend here is also a scholar." Al-Hakim chewed on a date.

Burns took out an Iraqi Dinar and handed it to the father. "One of the bags of crackers, please," Burns said.

The father attended to his business, handing Burns the bag of crackers.

"Yes, well," al-Hakim went on, "we are studying The Battle of the Camel and looking for historical sites associated with it."

The father still did not respond, nor did his wife.

The oldest boy however, fourteen years old, said, "I know where it was."

His father wrinkled his brow.

"Well, the battle took place in the whole of the valley," al-Hakim told the boy. "We are looking for specific evidence."

"Yes, but there are some pictures on the rocks there showing the battle."

Burns almost swallowed his soda down his trachea, coughing.

"You all right, Patrick?"

Burns said, "Yes." To the boy he said, moving in closer, "Can you show us where you saw these pictures?"

"It is too far and he cannot go," the father said.

"But I know where it is," the boy said to his father.

Burns pulled out a wad of Iraqi Dinar and peeled off some notes, equivalent to five hundred dollars. The father's eyes lit up, as this was a substantial amount, more than a month's wages.

"This is for now," Burns said. "I will match it with an equal amount when you show us the site." He handed the wad to the man who hesitated, but took it nevertheless.

The father considered the wad of bills in his hand. "We go," he said to Burns.

Burns and al-Hakim hopped into the Rover and followed the father and the boy in their dilapidated Toyota Tacoma. The Tacoma, followed by the Rover, retraced the route Burns and Al-Hakim had just driven. They drove for a few miles until they were back in *Wadi-us-Saba* area. They turned off the main highway and onto a dirt road alongside an escarpment. After two miles, the Tacoma pulled over. The boy got out and ran up along the escarpment. Burns and al-Hakim ran after him.

The boy crawled under an overhanging boulder and pointed at something.

Burns, then al-Hakim, knelt down and crawled under the overhang too. They discovered a series of petroglyphs chiseled into the rock, all protected from the elements and ages by the overhang. "These pictures are of The Battle of the Camel," said the boy, smiling.

Indeed, the two men saw dozens of markings all over the place depicting armies of men in battle. Some held swords above their heads and had apparently hacked one another because many markings showed headless people; their heads on the ground near their feet.

They also saw some similar markings they had seen both at *Al-Masjid al-Nabawi* and at *the Dome of the Rock*. They followed the boy and crawled out from beneath the overhanging boulder. Burns surveyed the *Wadi-us-Saba* in front of him. "Incredible," he said. "This is it."

The boy's father climbed out of his Tacoma and stood next to it. Burns handed the boy another wad of Iraqi Dinar and waved at the father. The boy ran down to him and together they departed in their truck.

The professors retrieved their backpacks from their Rover, trudged back up to the site, and crawled under the boulder again where they started to study the markings.

Chapter Twenty-Five

Colonel Mack strode into Graves' office. "Bob," Graves said from behind his desk. "Thanks for coming over."

Mack sat in a chair facing him.

"Listen, Cunningham is missing, abducted by al-Salah."

Mack shifted in the chair and sighed. "This have anything to do with Burns?"

Graves leaned in. "I have my team working on this twenty-four seven, but see what you can find out from your end. If you get a tip, I'll have the Iraqis handle it so we can plausibly deny it."

Mack raised an eyebrow. "Is Burns in danger?"

"We'll do everything we can to safeguard him."

"Dammit it, Jim. He's one of the best. His troops love him."

"I know, I know. But believe me, his assignment is a very important one that comes from the top. He has the potential to make a significant contribution to, well, history perhaps."

Mack frowned.

"Can you put your ear to the ground?"

"I'll see what I can come up with," Mack said. "I'll have DIA and CID get on it." He departed.

Graves was an expert at what he did, putting together black-operations. In Iraq, he normally used Iraqis aided by American forces. For this operation, however, they couldn't be trusted after Cunningham's disappearance at the hands of al-Salah. He might have to shut this thing down after all; that is, pull the plug on Burns and his professor friend if it continued to spiral out of control. He wasn't at that point, yet. He wanted this to play itself out just a little longer in the hope Burns could pull it off. Although, if it did continue to deteriorate, he would ensure in no way could it be traced back to him, the U.S. Army, the company, or the DCI.

The Iraqi father and his boy arrived back at their refreshment stand. They pulled in and saw a Mercedes SUV parked there. Three men, two shouldering AK-47s, saw them arriving and approached the truck. *He knew those two men he had just escorted could be trouble.*

"Your wife told us you took two men to a place in the valley," said the one young man without a right ear, lost in a scuffle with a rival gang as a child on the competitive tourist streets of Giza, Egypt. Nazim Qadir had shaved his long beard off, his hair now short. He had also discarded the Egyptian garb he had worn earlier when he sat in Yassim's apartment in Giza. He was now well dressed in a new tan *Cabela* long-sleeve safari shirt and matching cargo pants.

The father scanned the men's faces, then his wife's whose eyes grew wide. "We want no trouble," the father said.

"Then it is agreed. You will show us where you took them." Qadir did not have an AK, but did rest his hand on a Glock 9mm stuffed in his belt.

The father didn't need another visual to prompt him to comply. He climbed back into his truck and shooed at his boy who jumped out and ran to his mother's arms. The father drove off in his truck followed by The Brotherhood of Bakr, henchmen of Abdullah Nasir Yassim.

Chapter Twenty-Six

Al-Hakim made a notation on the map made by Ali's scribe to where they were in relation to the valley while Burns rubbed an etching paper on a section of the petroglyphs. The markings were similar to the ones they found in *Medina* and *Jerusalem*. They saw another depiction of a woman sitting on the back of the camel, but this one had a directional arrow pointing southwest.

Burns crawled out from under the boulder and calculated the azimuth in relation to the arrow on the engraving at about two hundred twenty-one degrees. He wrote it down in his notebook. He then studied the other etching. "What do you make of this depiction, Ahmed?" He handed the etching to him.

Al-Hakim examined it. "Well, it is a cube and could denote the *Ka'aba*," he said. "But what of this here?"

Burns inspected the marking again. "Perhaps a mountain? *Mount Arafat* is slightly to the east?"

Burns had been to the *Ka'aba*, which was the black cubicle shrine in *Mecca*, Saudi Arabia, believed to have been built by Abraham and his son, Ishmael, on the site where Adam built a house reflecting one in heaven called *al-Baytu l-Ma'mur*. *Mount Arafat* was east of *Mecca* where Muhammad gave his farewell sermon during his *hajj* and near where Abraham stoned the devil. It was also where Muslims believe Allah forgave the sins of Adam and Eve following their two hundred years or separation.

"But this marking here, farther northeast of *Mecca*," Burns said, pointing at it, "looks like a woman sitting under a half circle. This is open plains, and this is a rolling hillside." He moved his index finger over the map to show al-Hakim to where in relation the marking would be. "There's nothing there but desert."

Al-Hakim nodded. "Yes."

"The woman could be A'isha, as it looks similar to this one here of the woman on the back of the camel. This could be a cave near a hillside."

"It could be anywhere. There is no scale," al-Hakim said, looking out over the sandy desert.

Burns snapped some pictures of the area. They gathered up their packs and walked over to the Rover where Burns spread out the topographical regional map of Arabia on the hood of the Rover. They studied the features and locations.

Burns oriented the etching to the topographical map. He ran his finger along a line from where the *Ka'aba* was in *Mecca* to an area northeast of *Mecca* where it seemed the woman sat under the half circle in the middle of the desert near a hillside.

"There's nothing there," al-Hakim said.

"Let me calculate this new azimuth," Burns said. He took a map out of his satchel, the one he had drawn earlier with the V connecting

Jerusalem to *Mecca*, and *Jerusalem* to *Basra*. He used the azimuth he had just calculated from the directional arrow next to the woman sitting on the back of the camel where they were, and drew a line from *Basra* to *Mecca*. "Wow, look at that," Burns said.

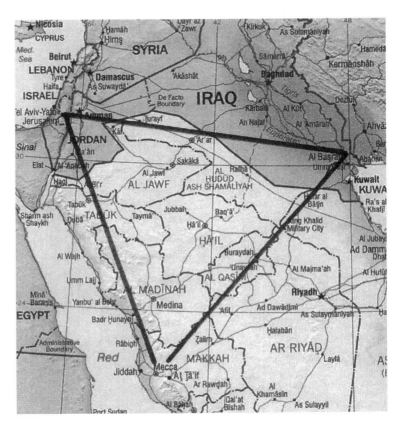

"It points right back down to *Mecca*, not *Medina*," al-Hakim said. "Huh. Wait a minute." He took out a travelers map and calculated the distance between *Jerusalem* to *Basra*, from *Jerusalem* to *Mecca*, and from *Mecca* to *Basra*. "What we have, Patrick, is almost equal distance between these locations, each slightly over twelve hundred kilometers. Perhaps our measurements are not quite accurate and it is exactly equal distance to the points being referenced. What we do have, however, is an equilateral triangle."

"That's certainly amazing, but what does it mean?"

"I do not know," al-Hakim said. Thinking aloud, he said, "An equilateral triangle has three equal sides."

Burns thought a moment. "Well, a triangle has exactly one hundred and eighty degrees. Equilateral triangles are essentially perfect geometric configurations."

He watched as al-Hakim tapped his finger on the triangle and looked from the triangle on the map over to the etching next to the map, then back again. "Wait a minute," al-Hakim said, searching around in the satchel and pulling out the loupe. He put it up to his eye, bent down and examined a marking on the etching. "Look at these markings here." He handed the loupe to Burns who stuck it into his eye socket.

Burns closely examined the markings on the etching.

"What do you make of that?" al-Hakim said.

"I never thought much of it before. They look like three small stars with another star in the middle."

Burns dug around in his satchel and pulled out the photographs he had taken at *The Dome of the Rock*. He also pulled from his satchel the etching from the Dome and compared that etching to the etching he had just made and the photographs he had just snapped. He found the exact same stars on the Dome etching and could make out, using the loupe, the stars on the photographs as well. He handed the loupe to al-Hakim who examined everything too.

Al-Hakim examined the same three stars on each artifact showing a triangular configuration, another star in the middle.

Burns used his pencil and connected the three outer stars on one of the etchings. What he had was an equilateral triangle.

The Lost *Hadīth*

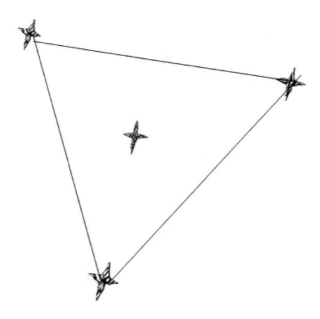

Al-Hakim studied the etching. "What do you think of the way in which they are tilted?"

"Yes. I see," Burns said. "Wait a minute."

"And what of the star in the middle of the triangle?"

"The incenter of the triangle?" Burns drew a line from the outer stars to the one in the middle.

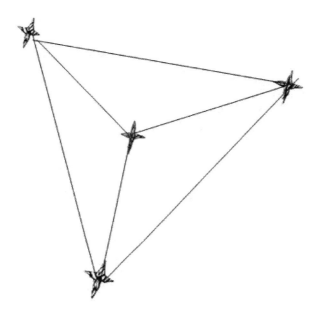

"My," al-Hakim said. "Look at these depictions again." He pointed to them on the etching. "We have the *Ka'aba* next to *Mount Arafat* and this marking of a woman sitting out in the desert in the middle of nowhere, just northeast of *Mecca*. She appears to be sitting under a half circle. I think the *Ka'aba* and *Arafat* are just reference points to *Mecca*, and this star denoting the incenter of this triangle of stars is important."

"Yes," Burns said. "The depiction of the woman under a half circle out in the desert on the etching is where the incenter of the triangle is. She's sitting where the incenter of the triangle would be on the map." He moved into place the map with the triangle he had just drawn. He used the straight edge of his notebook to draw a line to the incenter of the triangle on the map from all the three points, *Jerusalem, Basra* and *Mecca*. "*Jubbah,*" he said.

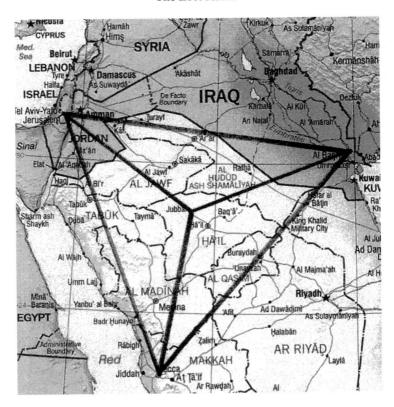

Jubbah, Saudi Arabia, Burns remembered, founded 7,000 years ago, was a small city near sandstone hillsides, most notably the *Jabal Um Sanaman*, the Two-Camel Hump Mountain in the *Nafud* Desert region. These sandstone hillsides seemed to pop up right in the middle of the desert.

"I do not believe it," al-Hakim said. "Why I did not think of this before. *Jubbah* is filled with thousands of petroglyphs thousands of years old and caves all along the sandstone hillside. The place has been crawling with archaeologists for thirty years now. I actually know one at Cambridge who has spent twenty years studying there." He paused a moment.

"What is it?"

"If this is where A'isha has hidden this *ḥadīth*, it most certainly has been discovered and probably by someone who never realized what they had, much like the Dead Sea Scrolls were almost lost, forgotten, and neglected." He studied the triangle on the map again, the three lines now connecting at the incenter of *Jubbah*. "Look at it from the top," he said.

Burns looked over the map from the top. "It looks similar to a pyramid," he said. "But a pyramid has four corners, this has three. Anyway, a triangle with this incenter suggests some sort of a perfect geometric configuration, as if to signify something. We know that Pyramids, especially for the ancient Egyptians, and many other cultures from the Mayans to the Greeks and others, believed mystically that pyramids helped mortals reach heaven. The deceased pharaohs could ascend the steps of the pyramid and reach the afterlife. Pyramids are perfect geometric shapes reaching up to the heavens."

"Perhaps A'isha constructed this whole affair for some sort of symbolic ascension," al-Hakim said.

"And everyone is wrong that this *ḥadīth* does not do what it is feared to do; rather it is meant for the opposite reason." Burns moved the triangle map around and considered it from different angles. "The way *Jubbah* is connected at the incenter of the triangle seems to show that each inner triangle could almost fold over onto the others in perfect geometric alignment."

"As if this so-called excluded or forbidden *ḥadīth* could help one reach heaven? Or enlightenment?"

Burns glanced over at al-Hakim and was glad he had said that and not him. What could be more enlightening, for Muslims, than what it is that they already had? "Well, then, we've come this far," Burns said.

"Yes," al-Hakim said. "I think we are near the end. This has to be where the *ḥadīth* is hidden. We have to keep going. We should go back to Cambridge and meet up with my colleague who has great knowledge on the petroglyphs at *Jubbah*."

In the distance, they saw the Toyota Tacoma truck fast approaching followed by the Mercedes SUV kicking up dust. "This doesn't look good," Burns said. "Let's go." They loaded up and hopped in the Rover. Burns started it up and, revving up the engine, peeled out and up the dirt road.

The father's truck pulled over to let the Mercedes pass. It tore after the Rover.

The chase now on, the Mercedes closed the distance on the Rover. On a straightaway, Qadir's henchmen lowered their windows and leveled their AKs outside. They each sprayed a burst of bullets from their rifles at the Rover.

Several rounds struck the Rover, blowing out the back window. Burns took evasive action and swung off in a new direction across a hard patch of dry dirt.

A cloud of dust spewed up at the Mercedes. This allowed the Rover to pull ahead by a considerable distance. Burns pulled onto a paved road and sped away. The Mercedes, a minute later, pulled onto the paved road as well and gained on the Rover again.

Just as the Mercedes came into firing range again, an American Apache Attack helicopter swooped over the Rover. It circled around and came up behind the Mercedes.

The men in the Mercedes stuck their AKs out the windows again and this time began firing on the Apache.

Several bullets whizzed past the helicopter. The Apache lifted up and dipped off to the left.

This distraction allowed Burns to pull away again.

The Apache swung around to the right of the Mercedes and rose higher into the air. It followed from this position so the AK men could not zero-in on it.

One of the AK men pulled himself up and out of the window and sat on the sill. He turned around and spotted the Apache high above them. However, just before he could squeeze off a round, the Apache's gunner, apparently not wanting to waste a more expensive Hellfire Missile, and considering he was relatively close to the Mercedes, let loose a volley of rounds from the Apache's 30mm automatic Boeing M230 chain gun.

Dozens of rounds penetrated the Mercedes causing it to swerve and roll over five times where it came to rest upside down on the hardened sand, a dirt cloud engulfing it. The two AK men were thrown from the vehicle.

"Angels from above, Patrick?" al-Hakim said as the Rover sped away.

"I think so," Burns said. They rounded a bend in the highway and came upon a roadblock of four American Military Humvees. Each Humvee had a M249 SAW, Squad Automatic Weapon, trained on them. Several soldiers had taken cover around their vehicles, their M4 assault rifles trained on the Rover.

Burns skidded to a stop. "Get out of your vehicle with your hands in the air," shouted an Iraqi interpreter in Arabic.

Burns and al-Hakim followed orders.

"Now get on the ground face down, your hands and legs spread out on the highway," the interpreter said.

They complied with the man's instructions. Four soldiers swarmed them while the others covered the event.

The soldiers patted them down and affixed plastic flexi-cuffs to their wrists. Two other soldiers searched the Rover, dumping their backpacks and going through their belongings.

"No weapons, Sergeant," said a young specialist.

"Get them on their feet," the sergeant said. The four soldiers standing guard over them helped them to their feet. The sergeant bent down and found their passports on the ground. He opened, scanned, then scrutinized them. He also glanced at their maps on the ground, markings all over them. "Burns and al-Hakim?" the young sergeant said in English, having realized their nationalities.

"Yes," Burns said.

"Yes," al-Hakim said.

"Why was that vehicle shooting at you, and our helicopter?"

"I am Professor Burns and this is Professor al-Hakim from the University of Cambridge. We're on an expedition." Burns decided not to tell them the truth to complicate matters. "Those men believe we've found some treasure. They're just trying to steal our find."

The sergeant squinted. "What, like Indiana Jones?"

"You could say," Burns said, cracking a smile.

The sergeant examined their passports again. "Egyptian and Canadian?"

"Yes," al-Hakim said, glancing over at Burns.

"Well, you're going to have to come with us until we can verify your story. You understand?"

Burns nodded. "We understand."

"I'm sorry but we have to keep you cuffed for our own safety until we get back to base camp." Burns was placed in one Humvee while al-Hakim was placed in another. Another soldier drove the Rover. The squad took off down the highway.

Three military Humvees pulled up to the overturned Mercedes

SUV. They found Qadir alive and administered first aid. Two soldiers checked on the two AK men and found them dead. The soldiers placed Qadir on a stretcher, tying him down. They searched the vehicle and found nothing of significance, except their weapons, which they confiscated. After placing Qadir in the back of one of the Humvees, they drove off.

Chapter Twenty-Seven

The young man in Paris working for al-Salah followed Sara and Jennifer along Avenue F.D. Roosevelt. He read a text on his phone:
Abduction set for tonight. Get the van and meet at the hotel.
He pocketed his phone and followed the young ladies for another block until they turned onto the Avenue des Champs-Élysées. He broke off his pursuit and disappeared down a side street.

Sara loved this city of lights. Paris was one of those cities, like New York, even New Orleans, that seethed life at all hours of the day and night. There was so much to see and do, and she had a whole two weeks to see and enjoy all that it had to offer. She also longed to see her father soon as she hadn't seen him since before his deployment last fall. She again thought of her mother and wished she could be with her now.

Colonel Graves leaned back in his chair while talking on his phone. A sergeant knocked on the open door, and he waved her in.

The sergeant handed Graves a manila file folder. The sergeant waited while Graves opened the folder and scanned the information there. "I gotta go," he said into the phone, sitting upright abruptly. From the file folder, he picked up and looked at a photograph of Burns and al-Hakim flexi-cuffed sitting at a table at a military outpost.

Burns and Al-Hakim sat flexi-cuffed at a table under a canvas on this hot Iraqi night. Two military police privates guarded them. A lieutenant approached, carrying the two men's backpacks. He set them down on the table.

They all watched as two MPs carried Qadir on a stretcher, placed him into an ambulance, and drove off out the gate. The lieutenant said, "Who's he?"

"An archaeological pirate," said Burns.

The lieutenant furrowed his brow. A military police captain approached the men. "Lieutenant," she said, motioning for him to come closer. Out of range, she whispered to him, "This is from the top. They're good to go. Give them their belongings and send them on their way."

"Yes, Ma'am."

The captain departed.

"Cut 'em loose, Private," the lieutenant said to one of the MPs. The MP cut their flexi-cuffs off.

Burns and al-Hakim rubbed their sore wrists.

"You may leave, gentlemen. The keys are in the Rover."

Burns and al-Hakim shot one another a glance but immediately grabbed their backpacks, hopped in the Rover, and drove off.

"I'll meet you here for breakfast in the morning," Jennifer said as she left Sara at her B & B. "Well, later this morning anyway," she said, flipping her mobile phone closed after glancing at the time. She walked off down the street.

Sara climbed the stairs to her room. The early Paris morning had cooled off, yet the room was still sticky.

Upon entering her room, two Iraqi men hiding behind the door grabbed her as she closed the door. One placed a rag over her mouth. She tried to scream, but whatever substance the rag had been dipped in, caused her to lose consciousness. Her body drooped forward.

One man draped her over his shoulder. They hurried down the stairs and placed her in an awaiting van.

The young man who had been tailing Sara since New Orleans drove the van after the two men jumped in. It sped off down the *Quai de la Tournelle* along the bank of the River Seine.

Burns and al-Hakim made their way back to Kuwait during the night and arrived early in the morning at the airport. After checking their passports and scanning inside the empty vehicle, the Kuwaiti military allowed them to enter. When questioned about the blown out back window, and a few bullet holes in the rear of the Rover, al-Hakim explained bandits or insurgents had attacked them and tried to steal it.

They returned the rental to the airport, filled out the insurance papers, and booked a flight to London.

While waiting for their flight, Burns reviewed his maps and the etchings he had made while al-Hakim read his biography on A'isha.

Burns pondered the significance of what they had found and now felt more than ever they may indeed have a good chance at finding the missing *ḥadīth*. His place in history might be set after all. With any luck, this professor of archaeology at Cambridge could assist. A text came through on his phone:

Professor Burns. This is Jennifer in Paris. I am at Sara's B & B. I was to meet her early this morning but she is missing. She left her phone, everything, and no one has seen her. I am really worried. Please help.

He jolted upright in his seat, knocking the maps and etchings off his lap and onto the floor. Al-Hakim said, "Patrick, what is it?"

Burns rapidly texted a reply:

Stay put. I'm on my way.

"Sara's missing in Paris," Burns said, gathering his belongings off the floor. "You go on to London, and I'll meet you there after I find her." He stuffed the maps and etchings into his satchel. "Here." He handed him the satchel. "Take all of this and get started." He sprinted over to the airline counter, changed his flight to Paris, a departure leaving in one hour.

Unable to sit, he paced, and his head raced. He realized this must be related to his quest for the *ḥadīth*. *These people are dangerous and might use her as a trade*, he figured. *They can have it.*

As he boarded his flight, he saw Fatima standing at the curb at LAX. He imagined her murder at the hands of her brother, Jamal. Now, lunatics, because of religious madness, might be holding his little girl. He had lost his wife, due to a blind and selfish pursuit of his career. Now, because of this undertaking, he had endangered his only daughter. It had taken him years to get over Fatima's passing, although actually, he never had. He would forever blame and never forgive himself. He had been so self-centered. If only he had canceled his appearance and acceptance of that silly academic award at the conference in Chicago, he could have been there in the hotel room when that little bastard had attacked her.

He also thought about how people have suffered throughout history because of religious artifacts and endeavors; hell, anything related to religion for that matter. He thought about all of the wars between the ancient Israelites and the Philistines. He thought of how the Christians went one way, during the several crusades, slaughtering everyone who didn't convert to Christianity, then the Muslims going back the other way, slaughtering anyone who didn't convert back to Islam. These slaughters went back and forth a few times over the centuries. He thought of the quests to find the Holy Grail. He thought about *Jerusalem*, an artifact in and of itself, in the hands of the Jews, then the Romans, then the Arabs, then the Christians, and back to the Arabs, then to the Turks, then the British, then the Arabs again, and finally the Jews. What a circle of events that had been!

His plane took off and headed for Paris.

Chapter Twenty-Eight

Two Mercedes SUVs pulled up to a *Sunni* Mosque in central Baghdad. Armed men poured out of each one. Two men stayed and guarded the vehicles while two others escorted al-Salah into the Mosque through the front door.

A man at the door ushered al-Salah and his bodyguards into a side room where Yassim stood waiting. "I thought it best we meet here," al-Salah said, "where you feel safe and can see that my intentions are genuine."

"I appreciate your care with safeguard," Yassim said. He motioned for al-Salah to sit. Al-Salah's bodyguards hovered aside him.

"We have a mutual concern," al-Salah said, "and I believe it best we see what we can do to make the outcome favorable to both our perspectives."

Yassim slowly sat opposite and calculated al-Salah's proposal. "Yes, but we are no longer interested in the necklace," Yassim said.

"Nor are we." Al-Salah shifted in his chair. "We both know this Burns and al-Hakim are making progress in their quest to find the *ḥadīth*."

"But, my dear Muslim brother," Yassim said, "the prospect of recovering this *ḥadīth*, if it is true, complicates our cooperation. You seek it. We seek it. It may be favorable to us, or it may be favorable to you. It could be very dangerous one way or the other for what it may or may not contain. Simply, if we see that it favors our cause, then we expose it as genuine. If the other way around, you know we would destroy it. And I am sure your intentions are closely aligned with ours."

"Yes," al-Salah said. "That is why I am prepared to discuss a joint investigative operation to understand its merits. Our scholars and your scholars would work together. That way no one can destroy it."

Yassim did not exhibit a reaction. He knew this arrangement would ultimately never work. One would not simply allow the other to either expose or destroy this ḥadīth. He decided to play along. He knew they needed each other, at least for the time being.

"I am prepared to make an offering to express my sincere desire to work together on this," al-Salah said.

Yassim nodded and waved his finger for him to continue.

"We now have Burns' daughter in our possession. It is not safe to bring her to Iraq. I need your assistance to hold her somewhere under your control in another country."

"I see," Yassim said.

"I think it best we convince Burns to continue his quest for this ḥadīth and when he finds it, to turn it over in exchange for his daughter, jointly of course." Al-Salah waited for Yassim to respond.

Yassim continued to play along. "Okay, my brother. This will work because Americans are weak when it comes to their faith over life. We understand there is nothing we would not sacrifice for Allah, including our daughters."

"Then we have an agreement?" al-Salah said.

Yassim nodded. "We do. But the exchange must take place with both of us present and the ḥadīth taken to a neutral location to study."

"That is acceptable. I will send information to you on the Burns daughter."

Yassim nodded once.

Stepping outside the Mosque, al-Salah whispered to one of his men there, "We have no further use for the major." Al-Salah crawled into his SUV, his two bodyguards next to him. The man al-Salah whispered to climbed into the other SUV. Al-Salah's SUV zipped off in one direction while the other SUV drove off in the opposite direction.

Having no life-threatening injuries, although considerably banged up, Nazim Qadir recuperated on his stretcher in an American field hospital while an MP guarded him. He struggled, but realized he was tied down.

When an American medical technician approached to check on his condition, Qadir scowled.

"Good, you're awake," the technician said. "Captain?" he called out.

"I do not require your assistance," Qadir said in a heavy accent.

The technician ignored him.

A female doctor approached. Qadir glared at her. "I do not want that woman attending to me," he said, turning his head away from her and back at the male technician.

"Oh?" said the technician. "Too late. She already saved your life."

"I do not understand you Americans."

The doctor reviewed Qadir's medical chart. "You should make a complete recovery," she said.

"Tell this woman I do not speak to women," Qadir said, continuing to stare at the technician.

"I have read that in the time of your great prophet," she said, "and even by his actions, women were revered and well-respected members of the community. Wasn't his first wife, Khadījah a well-respected and wealthy merchant?"

"You know not what you speak of."

She placed his chart on a hook next to his stretcher. "He can be moved now," she said to the technician. She said to Qadir, "And you are welcome." She walked away, leaving him simmering.

A few minutes later, the MPs transferred Qadir to a field ambulance. It drove out through the front gate and down the long dirt road followed by a MP Humvee.

Chapter Twenty-Nine

Burns checked his phone as he hustled through the terminal at Paris' Charles de Gaulle International Airport. A text came through from Cunningham's phone. He stopped to read it:

We have your daughter, Professor Burns. Do not look for her in Paris, but go about your quest. We will soon contact you for a trade for that which you seek.

He entered a response:

If you harm her in any way, you will get nothing. And what did you do with Cunningham?

He sent the message then hailed a taxi that took him all the way down to the Left Bank and to Sara's B & B. He paid his fare and rushed into the interior portion of the café where Jennifer sat waiting, her eyes swollen from crying. She jumped up to greet him. "I'm so sorry, Professor Burns." She wiped tears from her eyes.

"Can you show me her room?" They climbed the narrow staircase to Sara's room and he scanned it.

"I'm worried, Professor. I've heard how women are kidnapped, especially western ones, and sold into sex slavery in developing countries."

"I can assure you it has nothing to do with that. Can you gather her things and keep them for me?"

She nodded, sobbed and packed Sara's things.

"Look, Jennifer, this has nothing to do with sex slaves. I'll get her back." He pulled her close, hugging her and whispered in her ear, "I want you to go about your business and keep a low profile. Can you do this for me?"

She wiped her tears away. He released her and said, "Good." He hurried down the stairs and onto the street. He hailed another taxi. "To the Gar du Nord," he said to the driver. As he crawled into the back seat, another text came through:

> *Do not concern yourself with Cunningham. Only your daughter. We want that which your government has sent you to find, Professor. Do not look for her in France for she is already out of the country. If you do as we say, you will get her back alive. We will contact you.*

He entered another text in reply:

> *I will give it to you. I repeat, do not harm her! Alive is not good enough.*

He hit send and paid his fair at the station. He hopped out of the cab and burst into the Gar du Nord train station where he purchased a ticket on the next Eurostar to London, departing in half an hour.

Colonel Graves followed a sergeant down a dark hallway and through the doors of the U.S. military morgue in Baghdad. They approached a table, a body under a sheet. Standing next to the table waited Major Garrett. The sergeant lifted the sheet to expose the upper half of Major Cunningham's body. His forehead had a single bullet entry point.

Graves sighed and nodded at the sergeant who covered the major.

Garrett followed Graves out of the morgue. Graves stopped, turned and said, "I'd love to kill that bastard al-Salah with my bare hands." He pulled a handkerchief from his pocket and wiped a bead of sweat from his brow. "Increase the surveillance on al-Salah," he continued. "Locate Burns and keep close. Whatever happens, don't let that bastard get these damned writings!"

Garrett hustled off. Graves caught his composure and departed as well.

A large private yacht pulled up and docked in *Jiddah*, Saudi Arabia on the Red Sea. Three men on board escorted nine heavily sedated young women off the boat. The women's heads, covered by *hijabs*, their faces veiled, wore long black *abayas*. Their hands were handcuffed together on a chain. They walked toward a waiting van parked on the dock.

One of the men un-cuffed the ninth woman when they stopped at the van. He held her there while the other men loaded the remaining eight women into a van.

A man, waiting by the van, stepped forward.

"This is her," said the man who had un-cuffed the ninth woman, steadying her by the arm.

This man waiting by the van took her arm and led her to a sedan parked nearby. He had to hold her steady as well because she swayed and almost fell to the ground.

The man placed the woman in the rear seat where a small, fidgeting, middle-aged man sat. He had a very large and ugly scar across his right cheek from his ear to his chin. He wore a patch over his left eye.

The first man climbed into the front seat and turned to face the young woman in the back seat. "We should inspect the hostage to make sure we have the right one." He picked up a photograph of Sara Burns from the seat next to him. The scarred man in the back seat lifted the young woman's veil. Sara's drowsy eyes flickered slowly, her head swayed.

The scarred man sitting there in the back seat examined her. She seemed familiar to him in some sort of way. He stared at her knowing for sure he had seen her somewhere before, but couldn't be certain where. His greasy face twitched.

The man in the front seat glanced down at the photograph and up at Sara.

"Is it her?" the scarred man in the back seat said.

"It is." The man in the front seat put the photo back into the file folder and placed it on the passenger seat.

A bead of sweat rolled down the scarred man's forehead. Something about this young woman made his heart palpitate, not in a sexual way, but in a nervous way. "I wonder who she is," he said, "and why the Brotherhood wants us to hold her." He cocked his head and said, "Does not matter. We will fulfill our obligations and serve Allah." He lowered the veil over Sara's face, and they drove off towards *Medina*.

On the outskirts of Baghdad, the ambulance carrying Qadir sped along followed by the MP Humvee.

The vehicles turned down a narrow side street and headed towards a military prison. A car pulled out and followed them. The driver in the car talked into a mobile phone.

When the convoy came to an intersection, a van pulled into the ambulance's path. The ambulance swerved to miss the van and crashed into the side of a building. The Humvee swerved to miss the van and stopped short of running into the back of the ambulance.

The man in the car threw a percussion grenade out the window of his car. It went off near the MPs. Two ski-masked armed men toting AKs burst from the van and shot the two technicians in the front seat of the ambulance.

The two MPs in the Humvee, jolted by the impact of the grenade, began to stir. As they did, the two masked-men sprayed them full of rounds. The two masked-men extracted Qadir, who was stunned as well, and carried him to the van that sped off a moment later.

Chapter Thirty

Burns made his way down the hallway and into al-Hakim's office at the University of Cambridge and found him behind his desk. "Patrick," said al-Hakim, "this is Professor Winston Attlee, of ancient Middle Eastern archeology."

He rose to shake hands with Burns. Attlee was a distinguished English gentleman in his late sixties, grey beard, and full head of matching grey hair.

"Any word on Sara?" Al-Hakim said.

"Yes and no. She's been taken by the men who have been trying to steal the necklace and stop us in this quest. However, they will now only trade for the *ḥadīth* and will contact me after we've found it. I'm worried she is very frightened."

"We will give it to them," al-Hakim said without hesitation. "It is not worth anyone's life."

"What have we learned about *Jubbah*?" Burns said to take his mind off her situation.

Attlee handed Burns a photo album with several pages marked by post-it notes. "If you look at the photos I have referenced," Attlee said, "you will see I have found over the years a section that contains photos similar to the ones you have found in *Medina*, *Jerusalem* and *Basra*."

Burns studied the photos and turned the page to view some more.

"As the area of markings and rock art cover fifteen square miles," continued Attlee, "many of these finds you see here were only recently

The Lost Ḥadīth

discovered in the year two thousand and one by a Bedouin. We have only begun to investigate this area. So much has yet to be mapped."

Burns saw one marking depicting stars aligned in the same triangular configuration they found at both the Dome and the *Wadi-us-Saba*. Another showed the woman sitting on the back of a camel, and another showed the woman under a half-circle.

"There are thousands of petroglyphs in this area all over rocks," Attlee went on, "in crevices and openings we have only just begun to catalogue. There are many caves no one has looked in as well."

"So it is possible no one has found the *ḥadīth*." He scanned more drawings in the photo book. Some he did not recognize. "What of these other markings?" He pointed to one in particular that depicted a man looking upwards to the sky. He stood before another man who had wings. Rays of light shone down upon the man below.

"It is peculiar," Attlee said.

"Gabriel standing in front of the sun, or God?" al-Hakim said. "The good news, Patrick, is that Winston has been to this very area and knows his way around."

"I wouldn't want to put you in danger, Professor," Burns said to Attlee.

"Any friend of Ahmed's is a friend of mine," Attlee said, "and I will do anything I can."

"Thank you." He glanced at al-Hakim.

"Well, then," al-Hakim said, "we should get together a crew and leave posthaste. When can you be ready, Winston?"

"There are matters of expense."

"It's all covered," Burns said. "Spare no expense."

Attlee nodded. "Okay then," he said. "I have eager graduate students itching for adventure. I can have a crew together and be ready to leave in a few hours."

"Good," Burns said. A text came through on his phone:

Meet me at the end of the hallway under the stairwell if you wish to see your daughter alive again.

"What is it, Patrick?" al-Hakim asked.

"Sara." Burns jumped up and sprinted down the hallway.

Attlee's face tightened as al-Hakim jumped up and followed Burns. Attlee followed too.

Burns fast approached a man hiding in the shadows at the end of the hallway under the stairwell. It was al-Salah's Armani-dressed henchman, Tahseen Omar-Hamed. Burns approached him, thinking, *this guy again?*

"I know you speak Arabic," Hamed said in Arabic stepping out from under the stairwell. "I want to..."

Before Hamed could finish his sentence, Burns took him by surprise, punching him in the mouth. Hamed jolted backwards.

Burns jumped on him in a flash, grabbing him by his shoulders and shaking him.

"Where is she?" he said in Arabic.

Hamed did not answer as he licked at the blood in the corner of his lips.

"You harm one hair on her head," Burns said, grasping Hamed's lapel and balling it up in his fists.

Hamed's face turned ashen, and his head quivered.

"Where is she?"

"Safe," Hamed whispered.

"I asked you where." He punched Hamed again, this time in the gut. He crumpled over.

Hamed struggled to get his words out. "She's at a safe house. In *Medina*."

"*Medina*?" Burns bit his lip, thinking, *Medina again?* "As Allah, the Merciful, the Compassionate is my witness," he said, "I will kill you if you bastards harm her one bit. I want her back. Safe. Without a scratch."

Hamed stared at him, his face frozen in terror.

Burns pulled the necklace out from under his shirt. "I will gladly exchange this for her."

"You know we no longer want that. We want the *ḥadīth*."

"I don't have it, and don't know if I will find it."

Hamed did not say anything and did not move.

"Who are you working for?"

He hesitated. Burns cocked his fist to strike.

"Hasan Ali al-Salah. But Yassim and the Brotherhood of Bakr seek this as well."

Burns thought a moment. He knew all too well that both al-Salah and Yassim were cold-blooded killers, in the name of Allah, and would kill thousands or more for their perverted interpretations of Islam. He knew, therefore, they would not hesitate to kill Sara and others in their pursuit of this *ḥadīth*.

"We will only trade for the *ḥadīth*," Hamed reiterated.

Burns glanced back at al-Hakim and Attlee standing behind him. He turned back to face Hamed. "Whether I find this *ḥadīth* or not, I will expect my daughter back, unharmed. You understand?"

Hamed nodded.

"If I don't find this *ḥadīth,* you can have the necklace for my daughter. If we find the *ḥadīth,* you can have it. I get my daughter back, and we all walk away with something. Understand?"

Hamed nodded again.

Burns turned and passed the two professors. They followed him down the hallway.

Back in al-Hakim's office, Burns tried to relax and focus on the dilemma he now faced. His despair heightened on the word from Hamed that Sara was in *Medina*. This only made him more anxious and concerned for her well-being, both physical and mental. He was beside himself for allowing this to happen. He had wanted so badly to find this *ḥadīth* for the sake of history and his part in it, but now, because of what had transpired, it didn't matter. It worried him sick that she had been abducted and taken to *Medina*, Saudi Arabia, where his wife had been murdered! How would he get her out of Arabia after the exchange? She had no visa, no official entry papers. He'd have to get her to the embassy in Riyadh for some papers and a passport. Well, he'd worry about that after he got her back.

Chapter Thirty-One

Qadir, in considerable pain, struggled to sit up in bed. He focused his eyes, then tore bandages off his face and arms. An intravenous drip had been stuck in his arm. He tore that out too. An attendant tried to intervene, but Qadir brushed the man aside. He climbed out of bed and limped down the hallway of a house. He stumbled into a room where two men guarded Sara. Still covered in her *abaya*, veil and *ḥijāb*, she slouched on the sofa, her head resting against a pillow. Qadir scanned the room.

The man with the scarred face burst into the room a moment later and stood behind him.

"What is going on?" Qadir said.

"You are in a Brotherhood safe house in *Medina*," the man with the scarred face said. He bent over from the waist while putting his hand over his heart. As he stood upright, his hand made a sweeping motion to the floor and he said, "Bakr, the blessed Prophet's chief companion, our brother."

Qadir bowed, as best he could due to his bruised and sore body, approximating the bow the man with the scarred face had made. Qadir said, "May Allah keep and guide you until your sacrifice is called for."

The man with the scarred face said, "My name is Jamal. Our brother Yassim has given me your new instructions."

Qadir considered Sara in her stupor. "Who is this woman?"

"I have not been told, except to keep and guard her for an exchange for that which we seek. Come." Jamal motioned for him to follow.

Qadir hobbled after Jamal down the hallway.

Major Garrett stood outside a conference room in the U.S. embassy talking softly to Graves. "They abducted Burns' daughter," Garrett said. "In Paris. Intercepted communications confirm she's being held at a Brotherhood of Bakr safe house in *Medina*."

"Damn." Graves shifted on his feet. "That means they're going to ransom her for these writings, if Burns can find them." Graves paused as a general passed him and entered the conference room.

Garrett handed Graves a file folder. "You should read this," Garrett said. "It sheds more light on Burns and his wife, and why he'll gladly trade for his daughter."

Graves thought a moment, then whispered, "We can't let that happen. We need to get a fix on all of this and move in at the right moment. If the shit hits the fan, you need to clean it up."

Graves moved away from the door to the conference room to allow other officers to enter. "Get in there and find the Burns girl. The Saudis owe me. If Burns finds these writings, don't let al-Salah or Yassim get their fuckin' hands on them."

"Right," Garrett said. He zipped off down the hallway.

Graves ducked into the conference room and took a seat. As some general blathered on, he skimmed the file on Burns, his wife, and their daughter. In the file he learned how Fatima had been betrothed to an older, wealthy Saudi executive at the age of thirteen. He was fifty years older than she, had three wives who could no longer produce children, and wanted a young bride to procreate some more.

A major next to Graves disturbed his concentration when he stood up to give a report on logistics. Graves tuned him out, flipped a page, and continued to learn how Fatima ran away shortly after the engagement with the help of her older sister, Nafi'a, who had earlier suffered a similar matrimonial fate when she had been betrothed. Nafi'a empathized with her younger sister and helped her escape by way of an international aid organization where she was smuggled out of Arabia and taken to the states, adopted and raised in San Francisco. She later met Patrick Burns at the university.

After Fatima's escape, Nafi'a reported to her family that Fatima had been kidnapped. However, the family discovered a few years later Fatima was living in America, and had married Patrick Burns, a Catholic at that! In any event, Fatima's family never learned that Nafi'a had instigated this escapade. In the end, her father commanded Jamal that one day he must punish Fatima for dishonoring the family. Jamal took that to mean he must kill her, an honor killing.

Graves also discovered that Fatima was very bright, and within three years had learned English and graduated from high school two years before her classmates. She went on to San Francisco State University where she met Patrick Burns and received her degree in liberal arts. She went to work for the same international aid group that had smuggled her out of Arabia. She gave birth to their daughter, Sara, a few years after their marriage. Sara was identical to her mother. Graves paused and understood how Burns blamed himself for his wife's death after he read how she went off to see her dying sister in *Medina,* and he flew off to a conference to present a paper and receive a reward in Chicago. After her murder, Burns devoted his entire being to making sure Sara received the best education and attention she deserved.

He turned to the last page and found out how Burns, a Catholic, and Fatima a Muslim, ditched it all and had a non-denominational marriage. They raised Sara to have a universal understanding of all religions. They allowed her to choose her own path.

He closed the file and glanced up at the major giving the lecture. He tuned out his blather as well and worried Burns would indeed not hesitate to give these writings to al-Salah. Graves could not let that happen.

Burns, al-Hakim, Attlee and his two young graduate assistants, Jonathan Jacobs and Sadiq Salim, stood waiting to board their Riyadh-bound plane at Heathrow. Jacobs and Salim were both in their middle twenties and British. Attlee and his assistants checked in several bags of tools they used in archaeological excavation.

After settling into his seat on the plane, before takeoff, Burns sent a text to Cunningham's phone:

We are making our way to Arabia. Do not harm my daughter. I will find this ḥadīth and you can have it.

He hit the send button.

The text found its way to Cunningham's phone where it beeped on the table near al-Salah's henchman. He picked it up and walked over to al-Salah and said, "Master. A text from Burns."

Al-Salah nodded and waved his hand for him to proceed.

"Burns is on his way to Arabia. He will meet our demands."

Al-Salah nodded. After some setbacks, it now appeared to him that his new plan would work after all. "We need to prepare for our trip to Arabia," al-Salah said. "Make the arrangements." He waved the man away with the back of his hand.

Their plane touched down in Riyadh, Saudi Arabia. Al-Hakim made the rental car arrangements while Attlee and his assistants retrieved their bags from the baggage carousel.

They rented a Range Rover and drove northwest making it all the way to the town of *Buraydah*. They booked some rooms in the *Moevenpick Hotel Qassim* where they showered and rested for the night.

They didn't notice the Toyota sedan that followed them from the airport in Riyadh. The sedan carried one middle-aged man. It pulled up and parked across the street from the hotel. The man, dressed in typical Saudi garb, surveyed the area. He texted a message on his phone:

They are here, in Buraydah. I will let you know where it is they go.

The Lost *Hadīth*

Early the next morning, before the sun had risen, Burns and his entourage freshened up. They dressed in clean clothes, mostly cargo pants and walkabout safari shirts. The two graduate students wore loose-fitting T-shirts. They stood out, but bore resemblance to typical archaeologists from universities who traveled to *Jubbah* to study the petroglyphs.

They departed the hotel for *Ha'il*, a city in the *Shammar* mountain region, west of the *al-Odairie* valley. There they ate brunch. Attlee reviewed his maps of *Jubbah* and made some notations.

After brunch, they headed out of the city and traversed the road to *Jubbah*.

The man in the Toyota sedan, who had followed them from Riyadh, and now from *Buraydah*, continued to follow, keeping a safe distance.

Attlee drove the Rover, the desert surrounding them, all the way from *Ha'il* to *Jubbah*.

Jubbah, Burns read from the travel guide, rested near a large plain sixteen kilometers long and five kilometers wide, literally a city centered within an ocean of sand. The city was in a large ancient lakebed, perhaps once filled with water millions of years ago. A large sandstone massif overlooked the city and the lakebed. This is where, Burns learned, the vast inscriptions, rock art and other markings spread out over the mountain.

They drove off the main road and onto a dirt one running parallel to the sandstone mountain.

Attlee pulled the Rover over and parked near an outcrop at the end of a dusty trail. They waited for the sand and dust the Rover kicked up to settle before they got out. Attlee and his assistants grabbed their tool bags while Burns and al-Hakim clutched their backpacks. Burns also carried his satchel over his shoulder. He checked for any messages in reference to Sara, but found none. He reassured himself Yassim and al-Salah could not afford to harm her and risk not taking possession of this *ḥadīth*, but he had to hurry nonetheless. They could have this cursed *ḥadīth*. Hell, they could have the necklace as well.

They trudged up the side of the sandstone hillside. Attlee, consulting his notebook and the sketches he had made, led the way.

They saw the Lion of *Shuwaymus*, which was one of the largest of the petroglyphs in the area. All around the area were dozens of small to medium-sized crevices where one could crawl into. "This *ḥadīth* could be hidden in any of these," al-Hakim said to Attlee.

"They could," Attlee said, "but I have seen indications analogous to the ones you have found at *the Dome of the Rock* and near *Basra*. This way." He hiked up the hill and down a path.

They followed him and passed many animal images chiseled into the sandstone. Rounding a protrusion, they found more images and many unfamiliar symbols and shapes.

"Over here," Attlee said, continuing up the path. "I believe not far from here is where I saw your peculiar symbols."

Burns and al-Hakim followed Attlee, Jacobs and Salim, and trudged up an embankment and down another path. They climbed over rocks, through some large crevices and deeper into the mountain.

The man in the truck following them hung back on the dirt road near the Rover. He sent a text to his contact about where they went.

Chapter Thirty-Two

"Look here," Attlee said, trying to catch his breath.

Everyone stopped at an overhanging rock near some cotton shrubbery. Attlee pointed to several petroglyphs similar to those Burns and al-Hakim had found. Attlee's crew set their tool bags on the ground while Burns and al-Hakim surveyed the markings. They noticed the star dots that resembled the triangle, a star at its incenter. Near that, they saw the marking that resembled a woman on a camel, but no others. They did see the inscription in Arabic:

بكر انتقل الى رحمة الله طالك والدين السُمو
اطرب

"Bakr went to the mercy of Allah; now the *Suffah* hath showed," Burns said.

"This is similar to the one at the Dome," al-Hakim said.

"Yes," Burns said. "Yet, it has now become past tense."

"That could mean we have found the location." Al-Hakim looked around the edge of the large boulder and discovered other petroglyphs, but they mostly depicted animals.

Burns found a small opening behind an overhang not far from the big boulder.

Attlee's assistant, Salim, stepped forward. "Let me have a look." He knelt down and crawled on his belly into the opening. He wore a miner's helmet with an attached headlamp. He crawled in for only two yards then shimmied back out, legs first. "Nothing," he said. "Only walls with small animal etchings."

"There are other similar markings this way." Attlee motioned for them to follow him down the path. He led the way, the others following with their tools.

Hamed drove up in his rented Mercedes SUV and parked next to the man in the truck who had followed Burns and his crew to *Jubbah*. He climbed out of his rental and approached the man. Having discarded his Armani attire to blend in, he was now dressed in typical Saudi attire. "I am Hamed," he said to the man. He wore dark Armani sunglasses, however, to conceal his black eye.

"They are up there now, in the mountain," the man said, pointing towards the massif.

Hamed handed the man a wad of Saudi Riyal. "Your service is no longer needed."

The man drove off. Hamed returned to his SUV where he placed a call to al-Salah who called Yassim. He then drove back into *Jubbah* proper.

Qadir and Jamal guided Sara from the safe house to the waiting van. They tried not to grip her too tightly, because men were not allowed to touch a woman not their wives, mothers or sisters. Still fully covered in her Arabian garb, they placed her into the back of their Toyota van.

Although still feeling the effects of the drugs they gave her, she became more lucid because they had stopped drugging her.

Jamal continued to feel uneasy near her for some reason he could not explain. He was certain he had seen her, or knew her, from somewhere in his past. However, it was not his business to know who she was, or to question his brothers about her, yet he sweated more than usual, despite this being Arabia. They drove out of *Medina* and headed for *Jubbah*.

Chapter Thirty-Three

Attlee followed the bend in the path and walked around another large boulder where he came upon more markings. One, of a woman on a camel next to a man holding a sword above his head, intrigued him.

"This one is odd," Attlee said. "I did not think much of it the first time I had seen it, but they are facing away from one another."

"Yes," al-Hakim said, moving closer to examine it.

The Lost *Hadīth*

"It could be Ali with his back to A'isha," Burns said.

"I think you are right, Patrick. Look at this arrow, here." He pointed to one of those directional arrows, but this one was bent and pointing around the corner from where they stood.

Al-Hakim turned the corner and headed in the direction the arrow pointed. He walked a few paces and came upon some cotton shrubbery in front of the hillside. Above the shrub, he found the familiar triangle comprised of the stars and the incenter. Next to it, he saw what appeared to be the depiction of a woman sitting under a half circle.

Just above the two depictions, everyone saw what appeared to be a man sitting on the top of a mountain. Above the man on the mountain, the sun shone down upon him.

"This is like nothing we have found," al-Hakim said.

"Are you thinking what I'm thinking looking at that image?" Burns said.

"Muhammad up on the mountaintop? God shining his enlightenment down upon him? A'isha sitting in a cave?"

Below the markings, Burns brushed some of the cotton shrubbery aside with the back of his hand and discovered what appeared to be an entrance to an opening in the rock. A small boulder and other rocky debris blocked it.

"Looks as though it could have been a cave," Attlee said.

Burns and al-Hakim shot one another a glance. "Only one way to find out," Burns said.

"Let's do it," Attlee said to Salim and Jacobs.

Jacobs and Salim unpacked their excavation tools. They hacked at and detached the bush. They removed the smaller loose rocks around the larger boulder. Burns pitched in and helped move some of the rubble as well. Attlee and al-Hakim pitched a tarpaulin, in a lean-to fashion, not far from the activity.

After they had cleared away the smaller rocks, Jacobs and Salim dug under the boulder to create a ditch to jar it loose. It took some time. The hot Arabian sun above soaked them with sweat. Burns handed them water bottles from their packs and they drank heartily.

After they had rehydrated, Jacobs, Salim, Burns and al-Hakim all assisted in rolling away the boulder.

"Let me take a look," Jacobs said. He crawled into the cave. He only got a few feet before shimmying back out. "It's blocked by a small cave-in, but it appears to go deeper. I think we can dig through it, but the roof seems unstable. If we secure it, we might be able to go further."

"May be too dangerous," al-Hakim said.

Everyone thought a moment.

"I'll do it," Burns said. He noticed al-Hakim's worried face. "They're not going to settle for the necklace, Ahmed."

"There're more markings on the inside like the ones above," Jacobs said.

"This is it," Burns said to al-Hakim. "I have a strong feeling about this."

Al-Hakim sighed and nodded.

"If anything happens to me," Burns said, "give them what we have and get Sara out of here."

Burns scanned the faces of the other men. "Whatever we need to do, let's get on it."

"Right," Attlee said. "Well, then, we will need to find some wood chocks and supports to hold it up when we excavate the debris. I'll go back into town with Sadiq. Jonathan, you can slowly, and carefully, remove what you can."

Attlee and Salim hurried back down the path.

Jacobs took a small sandbag out of his excavation kit and tied one string on one end of it and another string on the other end of it, each string five feet in length.

He handed one of the strings to Burns. Jacobs crawled into the opening and wormed his way up to the blocked passage. He scooped up some sand and small rocks and placed them into the bag. When he had filled it, he closed the clasp and tugged on the string. Burns pulled the string at his end and the bag slid out. He opened the clasp and emptied the bag of dirt and rocks onto the ground. He then tugged on the string and

Jacobs pulled the empty bag back into the cave. He and Burns repeated the action several times.

Chapter Thirty-Four

The Rover, driven by Attlee, pulled into a junkyard, as no Home Depot, or the Saudi equivalent there in *Jubbah* existed. Although Saudi Arabia had modern highways and facilities, many small towns did not. Attlee chose this establishment because he spotted some discarded wood and other items that could possibly serve practical purposes in this endeavor. He spoke to the proprietor who bartered with him. Salim loaded some two-by-four boards and two-by-six boards into the back of the Rover. Attlee bought a small handsaw as well and they headed back to the excavation site in short order.

The van carrying Sara passed the Rover driven by Attlee, one going one way and the other the opposite. Qadir drove, and Jamal rode in the passenger's seat. Sara, in the back seat, continued to awaken from her stupor. They took her to a small home on the edge of town.

Attlee and Salim arrived back at the cave carrying as much of the wood as they could. Jacobs measured a two-by-four and cut it accordingly. Salim went back to the truck to get the rest of the wood.

Jacobs next cut a two-by-six. He took a small mallet out of his kit and crawled back into the cave.

Burns and al-Hakim spread another tarpaulin under the lean-to and placed rocks on its four corners to hold it down.

Salim returned with the rest of the wood and helped Jacobs fill the sandbag, sliding it back and forth several times. Burns kneeled down and peered into the cave to see Jacobs using the wood to secure the fragile roof of the cave. This went on for a half an hour until Jacobs shimmied back out again.

Salim took over and crawled in. Jacobs cut some more wood and passed it to him.

After Salim had dug for twenty minutes, he edged out again, his face lighting up. "I have broken through and the cave goes further. There is a chamber a few yards beyond that."

Attlee glanced over at al-Hakim and Burns. Burns nodded. He took out a clear, heavy plastic protective bag from his backpack and tucked it in his shirt. He lay down on his belly and crawled into the small cave.

Inside, he turned on the light to his miner's helmet. He crawled several feet into the cave and realized how confining a space this cave turned out to be. His hips barely cleared the sides of the tunnel. As he passed by the section where the cave-in had been, his foot brushed up against the roof support that one of the two young men had just made. One of the boards fell onto his leg. It hurt, but that was not what worried him the most. A considerable amount of sand fell onto the floor of the tunnel and onto his legs. He closed his eyes and put his head down until the dust had settled.

He realized he was lucky, thus far. It wasn't a total cave-in, but the sand now reached halfway back up to the roof of the cave near his feet. He shook the sand from his legs and continued crawling into the small chamber. The thought of entombment crossed his mind, but he had to push on.

The inside of the chamber was dry and dark. He adjusted the light on the miner's helmet and scanned the chamber. To one side he noticed a lump on the ground covered by sand. He inched closer to inspect. He brushed the sand off the lump on the ground and discovered it was actually a pottery jar, about two feet tall. It rested on its side. He noticed a ledge above and assumed the jar must have fallen off, probably by the same earth movement that had caused the original cave-in behind him. "Focus," he whispered.

He set the jar upright and opened the lid. Inside, he discovered four incredibly old codices, each about a foot and a half long by a foot wide and two inches thick. The codices were wrapped in linens, although the linens had considerably deteriorated.

He hesitated a moment, realizing the significance of finding this, then felt disgusted about turning it over to religious fanatics to destroy.

The codices had sturdy covers made of thin wooden strips coated in wax. The wood was frail, slightly splintered, but still held together. Using great care, he lifted the cover to one of the codices and saw that the pages inside consisted of a heavy parchment material, perhaps sheepskin. He remembered many early Islamic texts were written on Arabic paper. In fact, the first paper mills in the world were built in Baghdad in 794 AD. In addition, he recalled, early Arab Muslims developed a method to make a thicker sheet of more durable paper. However, these pages were made of sheepskin parchment, which meant these codices were probably made sometime in the 7th century. He lifted one page. It was frail, but held together, although the ends had split somewhat. The text on the first page was faint, but decipherable. He delicately closed the cover.

He opened his shirt and pulled out the plastic bag. He gently picked up the first Codex and placed it into the bag. He then lifted the second, the third and finally the fourth. He zipped the bag closed, encasing the four books in it. He could not stuff them into his shirt, so he had to shimmy out backwards while holding the bag out in front of him.

At the location of the partial cave-in, he kicked at the sand and pushed himself through. As he passed, more sand trickled down from above, *the sand in an hourglass*, he thought. He only hoped there was no literal semblance to that notion. He waited a moment for the dust to settle before pushing on.

He emerged from the cave. Al-Hakim, Attlee, and Jacobs stood at the entrance eagerly waiting, Salim kneeling and helping him out. As he turned over onto his back, he handed the bag up to Salim who took it and passed it off to al-Hakim, whose face was frozen, his mouth slightly open.

Burns stood up and dusted himself off. Al-Hakim turned around, knelt down and gently placed the bag on the tarp behind him. He sat down on the tarp and stared at the bag.

Burns sat beside him.

"Could this be?" al-Hakim said. "Could A'isha have been the last person to have touched this?"

Burns nodded. He checked his phone: no text from the kidnappers. He gulped a hearty sip of water and said, "Now, let's see what we've found."

Chapter Thirty-Five

Al-Salah's SUV made it across the Iraqi border without incident; one of his bodyguards drove. It was a clandestine undertaking, and because he was a prominent *Shiite*, he had to travel undercover because Saudi Arabia was a *Sunni* country. He made arrangements, bribed the border authorities, and concealed his identity. He and his two henchmen all wore traditional Saudi garb to blend in. He listened to Hamed speaking on his mobile phone: "They have the Burns girl in *Jubbah*. The Brotherhood moved her there into a safe house today. I have also confirmed that Burns and his men are excavating up in the mountains."

"Good," al-Salah said. "We shall be there soon." He closed his phone and smiled. Soon he would have possession of this *ḥadīth* and could have it analyzed to either discredit A'isha, or destroy it to protect the faith. The SUV drove off and headed towards *Jubbah*.

Yassim deplaned from his commercial flight in Riyadh. A member of the Brotherhood waited and whisked him away in a sedan. They headed out of Riyadh and drove towards *Jubbah*. He was so close to getting his hands on this *ḥadīth*. Soon, he would be able to vindicate A'isha and her father, the great Abu Bakr, and destroy, finally, al-Salah and his misguided *Shiite* brothers.

Burns spread the four codices out in front of him on the tarpaulin while Attlee, Salim and Jacobs surveyed and documented the inside of the cave, as far as was safe. They cataloged the area and made notations in their notebooks.

The first codex translated as *The Question,* the second *Acceptance,* the third *Rejection* and the fourth *Dissension.*

The first order of business centered on photographing each page. Al-Hakim had a high-powered camera on a tripod he placed squarely over the first codex. Gently, Burns opened the cover. The parchments in each codex were stitched together by frayed heavy thread.

Al-Hakim snapped the first picture and checked to see its quality. He readjusted the setting and reshot the picture. He readjusted it one more time and retook the picture yet again. He then nodded to Burns who delicately turned the page.

Al-Hakim snapped a photo of each page. This went on for several minutes until he had photographed the four codices.

He disassembled his camera and tripod and packed them away in his backpack. Burns set aside the first codex, *The Question*, from the others and opened the cover.

Al-Hakim read in Arabic:

This is the sahih, the true accounting of the Prophet Muhammad; Sīrah Rasūl Allāh, Life of the final Messenger of Allah, as I have beheld, A'isha, thy Prophet's wife, his confidant, a mother, a believer.

He glanced over at Burns who nodded and turned the page. Al-Hakim read the second page:

Husband, troubled by his own people's polytheistic idolatry, rampant; Husband, troubled by his own people beholden to falseness; Husband, troubled by his own faithless people; Husband, troubled by his own people adrift. And the Jew hath faith, Husband cried; and the Christian hath faith, Husband cried; Husband, troubled by his own faithless Arab brethren without a path, without enlightenment.

Al-Hakim sighed and looked at Burns as he turned the page:

A great time hath now passed; a great time Husband hath been troubled; a great time Husband hath wrestled with this question, one of faith; a great time Husband hath been weighted down by this question; a great time Husband hath been burdened by this question of faith; a great time Husband hath been agitated by a lack of faith, of his own people; Husband hath labored with great questions, of his own people, faithless.

Burns swallowed hard and turned to the next page. Al-Hakim continued reading:

And hence, visions came upon him, Husband, in dreams; and hence, visions of faith came upon him in dreams; and hence, visions of account of all that hath been before, in dreams came upon him; and hence, visions of accounts as told by others, the Jew, the Christian came upon him; and hence, visions now to be held for thy brothers in context for perfection came upon him; and hence, visions, on His behalf, Allah, as announced by His messenger, Gabriel, came upon him, Husband.

He frowned and said, "So there is nothing outside of what has been known, Patrick."

Burns nodded and turned the page. Al-Hakim continued reading:

Each vision, in a dream, questioned by him, Husband; each vision, in a dream, debated deeply within by him, Husband; each vision, in a dream, troubled him, Husband; each vision, in a dream, challenged him, Husband, to ponder his validness; each vision, in a dream, hath been spoken to thy Prophet's companion, wife; each vision, in a dream, hath been examined with thy Prophet's companion, wife.

"My lips are parched," al-Hakim said, his hand trembling slightly as he found a bottle of water in his backpack. He took a swig and continued:

Thou art not mad, Husband, thy wife cried; Thou art not troubled, Husband, thy wife cried. Whilst thou dreamt, thee trembled, pitched to and fro; whilst thou dreamt, thee became sodden with perspiration; whilst thou dreamt, thee became frightened, yes; whilst thou dreamt, thee became fearful of that which cometh upon thee, from visions, in dreams.

Al-Hakim glanced over at Burns and took another swig of water:

And in thy moment of doubt, in thy moment of uncertainty, thy companion, wife, comforted thee; thy wife swayed thee; made clear to thee; declared to thee; defended thee; brought thee back from thy verge of despair; wife helped thee see the light.

Burns turned the page.

And in thy moment of distress thy wife reassured thee; thy wife brought brightness; and in thy disbelief, thy wife convinced thee to accept thy purpose; and in thy desperation, thy wife cradled thee in her bosom, comforting thee to completeness.

"What do you think?" Burns said to al-Hakim as he closed this codex.

"I think it is clear more than ever how influential she was in his acceptance of himself as a prophet. As you know, there has been much debate as to her role and influence in this matter, but this, according to her, makes it profound."

Burns placed aside the first codex and opened the second, *Acceptance*. Al-Hakim read from it:

Husband, he hath now clarity, from visions, from dreams; now he hath in his heart trouble no more; now he hath doubt no more; now he hath no question in his heart no more; now he hath no question of self no more; now he hath accepted His revelation. And so adrift he art no more.

Burns turned to the next page.

Husband declareth that He above hath pronounced that the Jew held there is but One; Husband declareth that He above hath pronounced that the Christian held there is but One; Husband now declareth that He above hath confirmed hence, that the Arab, too, must hold but One; Husband now declareth that He above hath confirmed there is but One for the Arab, the Jew, the Christian; husband now declareth that He above hath given him, husband, visions, in dreams; Husband now declareth that He above hath held to him, Husband, that this religion, His religion, has always been held; Husband now declareth that He above, who hath now given him, Husband, His final revelation, is to rebirth it for His people.

Using a handkerchief, Al-Hakim wiped sweat from his brow. Burns turned the page.

Husband now declareth that He above hath held that the Arab must submit to but The One; Husband now declareth that he below, Husband, is one who now submits; submission to The One, Allah; in proper, Islam. Husband hath now proclaimeth that Allah, The One, hath perfected our religion for us; Husband hath now proclaimeth that Allah, The One, hath now completed his blessing upon us; Husband hath now proclaimeth that Allah, The One, hath now approved Islam as our only religion.

Al-Hakim looked over at Burns and cleared his throat. He gulped more water. Burns turned to the next page.

It followed that Husband now assembled His final revelation upon visions, from dreams; it followed that Husband now fostered faith, for his own people, from visions, from dreams.

Burns began to understand why Bakr probably might have excluded this *ḥadīth*. Some would certainly misconstrue it. As Jesus, who was purported to have said on the cross, 'Father, why hath thou forsaken me?' some would question these passages as to why Muhammad had questioned himself, as to why he had questioned his visions, as to why he had questioned his purpose, if he was always meant to be The One.

Al-Hakim continued reading from the next page after Burns turned to it:

It followed that his own people challenged him, Husband, and his visions; it followed that his own people challenged his assertions that he, Husband, is the Final Prophet; it followed that his own people pronounced that he, Husband, was false; it followed that his own people pronounced that that which they have is all that they need; it followed that his own people fought with him, Husband; it followed that he, Husband, worked under difficult times to convince his own people of His message, and of his purpose.

Burns turned the page.

At that time, at great length, wife convinced Husband to accept the challenge; at that time, at great length, wife worked under difficult times beside Husband to convince his own people of His message, his purpose, his task, as given by Him, The One, Allah, above, through His messenger, Gabriel.

Burns closed the last page to this codex. Al-Hakim stood up to stretch his legs. He wiped some more sweat from his brow using his drenched handkerchief.

Burns stood up beside him, took a swig of water from his bottle and, knowing full well, that deep down, his friend al-Hakim was a Muslim, inquired gingerly. "What's your impression, Ahmed?"

"I do not think we have found anything damaging."

"I agree. I think at this point this confirms much of what many, through the centuries, have theorized."

"Yes." Al-Hakim shifted his weight.

"That he questioned his visions and dreams."

Al-Hakim finished his bottle of water.

"And," Burns said, "the last passage reminds me of Jesus' own people challenging him. He was troubled by the rabbis who were more concerned with Old Testament practice than God's true message of compassion. Jesus didn't advocate a new religion, just a new way of understanding and finding God."

"Right."

"And him preaching at the *Temple Mount* where the rabbis challenged him. His own people, for the most part, rejected him as well."

Al-Hakim nodded and said, "Yes, there has always been a question of Muhammad's own feelings of worthiness and his acceptance as Allah's Prophet, and questions centering on his revelations which were borne as a direct result of his own people's continuance with polytheistic idolatry. In all religions, it is one's own faith that is the cornerstone. Faith is the foundation of all religion. Messengers, whether Moses, Jesus or Muhammad, are only vessels."

Burns nodded and drank some more water.

"Well, shall we continue?" They sat on the tarp and Burns moved the third book, *Rejection*, into place. Al-Hakim said, "This one sounds troubling." He read:

Husband now proclaimeth there must be augmentation of The One as held by the Jew; Husband now proclaimeth there must be augmentation of The One as held by the Christian; Husband proclaimeth there must be augmentation to confirm credence, for his own people; this shall be the word; the word of the One, as revealed in visions, from dreams.

Burns turned the page.

Husband held, this augmentation, be it known: the final revelation, from visions, in dreams; the final revelation of The One, as held by Husband, who hath received the final revelation shall recite now, the final revelation to all; be it known, al-Qur'an.

Burns thought about this. He knew that *al-Qur'an* literally meant, in Arabic, the recitation; and the compilation of this recitation of the final revelation, al-*Qur'an*, came much later. The *Qur'an* was actually dictated aloud by Muhammad to his companions who were required to memorize the recitation of the final revelation, *al-Qur'an*. In fact, thousands of Muhammad's followers were required to memorize it. As a result, different communities in the burgeoning Islamic world, because of differing dialects, recited passages differently. Abu Bakr assembled the first compilation of the *Qur'an*, but finally Uthmān ibn 'Affān, the third *Caliph*, made several copies of Abu Bakr's *Qur'anic* compilation. Uthmān then ordered all other differing texts at the time burned. However, Burns reiterated to himself, it was Abu Bakr who made the first compilation that would eventually become the *Qur'an*. A'isha's father was probably the most significant influence, after Muhammad and his wife, A'isha, in the development of not only the *Qur'an*, but the ministry itself.

Al-Hakim read from the next page:

Oh Jerusalem, we have prayed, Husband declareth. Husband, who hath received this al-Qur'an proclaimeth behold, he, Husband, be a prophet; Husband proclaimeth that he is His Final Prophet; cometh Abraham, cometh Moses, cometh Jesus, cometh Muhammad; save for the Jew, he hath come; save for the Jew, he hath been declared His final prophet; be it false, proclaimeth the Jew. Therefore, he, Husband, who hath received al-Qur'an, hath received another revelation from the One above, Allah, who commands Mecca, we now pray.

Burns glanced over at al-Hakim, who sighed, then turned the page.

Husband declareth that He above, Allah, now commands for the Arab, the true religion, submission to Allah, Islam; Husband declareth that Allah commands for all, the Jew, the Christian, His true religion, submission to Allah, Islam; Husband declareth that Allah commands that all shall fall, prostrate, for Allah now commands that Mecca, we now pray. He, Husband, who hath received al-Qur'an, shall preach therein. He, Husband, shall lead them to Mecca; for upon Mecca, which is blessed, as the House of Adam, as the house of Abraham, shall be from henceforth where he, Husband, shall lead.

Burns wiped sweat from his brow using his sleeve. Al-Hakim opened another bottle of water and took a sip. He continued reading from the codex after Burns had turned the page:

Husband now proclaimeth therefore, be it known to all others, not in submission to Allah, as such be it Islam, hence to be nonbelievers; that those not in submission to Allah, as Islam, cannot become righteous. Without conversion, all others, therefore, he, thy Husband exclaimeth, are forsaken by Allah.

Burns closed the back cover to this codex. He set it aside. "What're you thinking, Ahmed?"

"I am not sure I believe this with my own eyes," he said, taking yet another gulp of water from his water bottle.

"I understand your sentiment." Burns placed the last codex, *Dissension*, in front of him.

Al-Hakim nodded at him and said, "Okay." Burns opened the last codex and al-Hakim began reading from it:

Husband, who hath now received al-Qur'an from Him, Allah, as the last and true Prophet, went forth to proselytize his people. His people questioned him; his people challenged him. His people cried: He was an orphan, not of nobility. His people cried: He is a simple Bedouin. His people cried: He is an unlearned man. His people cried: He is no prophet.

Burns peered over at al-Hakim and turned the page. Al-Hakim continued:

Husband hath now labored many years in a great effort to convert his own people from polytheistic idolatry. Husband hath fought enemies of Allah and His true religion, Islam. Husband hath cast out demons inherited over the centuries by his own people. Husband hath cast aside those who hath rejected His, the One's, Allah's, al-Qur'an. Husband hath destroyed enemies who hath challenged him.

Al-Hakim read from the next page:

After great misfortune; after searching and questioning; after much doubt about visions, from dreams; after wife hath assured him; after acceptance of visions, from dreams; after repudiation by the Jew; after proselytization and conversion of his own people, he, Husband, hath now the religion that always hath been, Islam.

Al-Hakim read from the next page:

He, Husband, who hath received His al-Qur'an said: go forth my brothers, be not in conflict with one another upon my passing, for Allah will be displeased with thee; no division shall live; no disagreement shall be at hand; it shall not stand.

"There it is," al-Hakim said. "That could be the one particular passage she thought would hold sway over Ali."

"Perhaps," Burns said, turning the page. Al-Hakim continued reading from this last codex:

Husband held that his brothers will displease Allah if strife for control of his ministry shall arise. Husband held that his brothers must not put strife in play and must set aside differences; for Allah will be displeased, Husband held, if strife amongst his brothers grew; usurpation shall displease Him.

"Well, it does seem more neutral here," Burns said, "that both sides could have been guilty of the division."

"Yes. Division is inevitable with mankind due to interpretative practices. When does man agree on anything?" Al-Hakim read from the last three pages of the last codex:

I.

A Codicil, as written by A'isha, Umm al-mu'minin, companion, confidant, wife of the Prophet Muhammad.

II.

Bakr went to the mercy of Allah, yet the Suffah hath now showed unto you a path thou hath followed which has led to the incenter of a polygon, led by the stars, the light, above, upon which thee now stands, which this ḥādīth hath been laid upon. This ḥādīth is thine instrument to reach enlightenment, truly, in this matter before thee.

Bakr, thy great Caliph, father, companion to the Prophet Muhammad, hath set aside this ḥādīth; hath set aside this ḥādīth on presumption that a great disturbance be held, if it so be known; disagreement of its connotation. Daughter disagreed.

III.

Daughter of Bakr hath not destroyed this ḥādīth as father instructed. Daughter hath concealed this ḥādīth in preservation of recordation; recordation of Husband's travails as witnessed by daughter of Bakr; Daughter believed greatly in truth. Daughter, and thy daughter's husband, believed greatly in mankind to understand all that there ever was, or will ever be, and to have truth to weigh upon. Therefore, daughter hath left indication for only a worthy and penitent one; one who seeks truth; one who may know forgiveness; one who has Allah, and his kingdom, within him. Hence, this ḥādīth before you is for conclusion and inclusion, for elucidation, for enlightenment and for accounting. Faith hath inspired it.

Burns closed the last codex and set it atop the others. He and al-Hakim sat there staring at them.

Al-Hakim finally broke the silence and said, "What do you think about those last lines, Patrick?" He waited for a reply.

"Which ones?"

"A worthy and penitent one?"

Burns sighed, stood, and walked over to a nearby cliff. He could see *Jubbah* in the sandy distance. Al-Hakim frowned and walked over and stood next to him. "I don't know, Ahmed," Burns said, his voice cracking.

"Patrick?" Al-Hakim furrowed his brow and narrowed his eyes.

Burns turned towards him. "I just had the strangest feeling. Right now. Right here in my heart." He clutched his chest.

"Are you okay? What is it?" Al-Hakim put his hand on his shoulder.

"I was, well, I just thought, I don't know. I was reminded of Fatima just now. I mean, A'isha, she reminded me of Fatima." Feeling dizzy, he leaned against a large boulder.

Al-Hakim tried to steady him. "I understand. A'isha and Fatima were much alike. Both very smart women who felt deeply about truth, about love, and about forgiveness."

Burns looked over at him. "It was as if my heart just stopped beating, and was totally empty of blood."

Al-Hakim took him by his arm, but Burns slid to the ground and sat there clutching his abdomen. Al-Hakim sat down next to him.

"It's my fault she's dead, Ahmed." He closed his eyes, tears welling up.

"Fatima? But her brother, Jamal, killed her."

Burns drew in a deep breath and slowly exhaled. A tear dropped from an eye.

"You have never gotten over it, have you, Patrick?"

Burns kicked at a rock. "We quarreled just before she left. I really didn't want her to go, but she insisted. I told her it was too dangerous, that she was essentially a fugitive from her own family."

Al-Hakim studied him closely.

Burns wiped the tear from his cheek. "Well, she was going with or without me saying her sister was the only one who had understood and supported what she had done; running away. She said she owed it to her, and she had to see her again before she died." He folded his arms across his chest, as if to hug himself.

Al-Hakim held him by his arm.

"She begged me to go with her, Ahmed." He looked over at him. "To see her dying sister on her deathbed! For her husband to be with her." Another tear dropped from an eye onto his cheek. "I said no!" He sniffled, wiping that tear away too. "I said I had to go to Chicago, for the conference, for my career." His eyes bore through al-Hakim. "Her sister was dying! How could I do such a thing? Let my wife go and be murdered at the hands of her brother?"

Al-Hakim squeezed Burns by his arm.

"I told her she would have to go without me." He stood up and looked down from the cliff to the sandstone floor thirty feet below. "That stupid lecture at the University of Chicago and that silly award. Was it worth my wife's life?" He turned to face al-Hakim who stood up. "I put my career on the same, no a higher level, than my wife's life? How could a man do such a thing?"

"You had no idea this would happen," al-Hakim said.

"But it did. I went to that damn conference, and Fatima went to die at the hands of her brother. I should have been there with her, to protect her. Isn't that what a husband is supposed to do? Protect his wife?"

Al-Hakim put his arm around him as another tear fell onto his cheek. "It is not your fault, Patrick. It is Jamal's fault. Allah will judge him accordingly, not you."

"I'd like to believe that, Ahmed. But I can never forgive myself." He turned away from him. "She was the only woman I have ever loved in this whole insane, Allah forsaken world."

Al-Hakim rubbed his shoulder. "You see, Patrick? You *are* the worthy and penitent one."

He sniffled and wiped more tears away.

"Only a humble, penitent one can enter the kingdom of heaven, Patrick."

Burns chuckled. "You sound like my priest." He sniffled again and walked back to look down at the codices, al-Hakim following.

"Now," Burns said, "because of this fool's errand, because of blind ambition in search of the lure of ancient secrets, I left my troops back in Baghdad, maybe even to die without me, because I have been duped into looking for this lost, hidden, or forbidden, whatever you want to call it, *ḥadīth.*" He turned as al-Hakim pulled up next to him again. "And they have the only other person I have ever loved; my daughter."

They stood staring at the codices for a long moment. Al-Hakim turned to face him, put his hands on both of his shoulders, and peered straight into his eyes. "This *ḥadīth* is not worth Sara's life. They can have it. We will exchange it posthaste."

"But what do you make of all this, Ahmed?" Burns waved his hand over the codices below him.

"Nothing. No one would believe this. Besides, what do they show except Muhammad questioning who he was? That A'isha was instrumental in convincing him to accept these visions and his dreams? That A'isha convinced him to preach this final revelation as he believed he was instructed through his visions? That he fought his own people to get them to abandon their polytheistic ways? That the Jews rejected him, and that Muslims and Jews have had hatred between them for centuries because of their religions differences." He paused and said, "As you know, all of the *aḥādīth* are interpretive, all religious texts are. I see it one-way, you see it another. Hence, the *Sunni* and the *Shiite*. Hence the Catholic, the Protestant, and the Jew. Scholars would fight over what this means for decades, generations."

Burns nodded and pursed his lips.

Al-Hakim patted him gently on his shoulder and said, "Well then, let us go and get Sara back."

Chapter Thirty-Six

A Hummer H2 raced across the porous, open boarder of southern Iraq and into northern Saudi Arabia. This was where coalition troops had dashed into Iraq both in the 1991 Gulf War and in Operation Iraqi Freedom in 2003.

Inside the Hummer four American men in civilian clothes, each sporting an Uzi sub-machine gun on a sling around his neck, and a 9 mm Beretta sidearm, rode along. They wore Iraqi scarves around their necks so they could pull them up over their faces if needed to conceal their identities. The one man in the backseat, Major Garrett, reviewed a map of the *Jubbah* area. His phone rang. He answered it, "Garrett." He listened a moment and wrote some numbers on the edge of the map. "Got it," he said into the phone, tearing off the section of the map he had just written on. He handed it to the man in the front passenger's seat. "Here're the coordinates."

The man entered the coordinates into the GPS device on the dashboard.

The sedan carrying Yassim drove into the front yard of the safe house in *Jubbah*. He crawled out as Qadir emerged from the house carrying an AK-47, the butt resting on his hip. Jamal stood in the doorway gripping an AK across his chest.

Al-Salah and his two bodyguards pulled up onto the front yard of the safe house a minute later. Hamed sat there waiting for him in a parked car across the street. He climbed out when he saw his boss pull up and park.

Al-Salah got out of his SUV. His bodyguards un-shouldered their rifles and surrounded him.

Yassim held his hand up to reassure Qadir. Yassim and al-Salah met in the middle of the yard. "We have an understanding," Yassim said.

"We do," al-Salah said. "Notify Burns," al-Salah said to Hamed. "We are ready for the exchange when they have found the *ḥadīth*."

Hamed punched a text into his phone.

Burns, al-Hakim, Attlee and his boys packed up their equipment and made their way back down the path to the Rover. While loading up, the text came through for Burns:

We are here in Jubbah for the exchange when you have found that which we require. Exchange at 27E al-Hail Street.

Burns entered a response:

We have found what you are looking for. I only want my daughter.

"This is it," Burns said. "Let's go."

Al-Hakim nodded. They finished loading the Rover and drove back into town.

Chapter Thirty-Seven

The Rover drove up to the safe house and stopped on the side of the road across the street. Burns jumped out followed by the others.

Qadir and one of al-Salah's bodyguards waited in the front yard. They raised their weapons at Burns.

"We have no weapons," Burns said in Arabic. He and the others stood in front of the Rover.

Yassim, Hamed, al-Salah and his other bodyguard came from the house and approached Burns. "You have the *ḥadīth*?" al-Salah said.

"We do," Burns said, holding up his satchel. "I need to see Sara."

Al-Salah nodded at Yassim. Yassim called out, "Bring her out, Jamal."

Burns watched as Jamal emerged from the house holding Sara firmly by her arm. He carried his AK-47 in his other hand. He took a few steps from the house and froze in his tracks upon seeing Patrick Burns standing before him.

Burns could not believe whom he saw standing there in front of him holding his daughter. He noticed the very large and ugly scar across Jamal's right cheek from his ear to his chin that his wife had made in the throes of death. Jamal also wore an eye patch where Fatima had poked his eye out during the struggle. "Jamal?" Burns said.

Jamal loosened his grip on Sara, turned, looked at her, and abruptly tore her veil from her face and her *ḥijāb* off her head. "Fatima?" he said to Sara.

Sara, still a little sluggish, looked at her father in the yard before her. "Dad?" She started staggering towards him.

"Sara!" He started for her.

Jamal lunged forward, grabbed her by the arm, pulling her back.

Burns threw his satchel into the air. It landed near the feet of al-Salah and Yassim.

Jamal leveled his rifle at the fast approaching Burns and squeezed the trigger.

A burst of rounds impacted near Burns' feet. He hit the ground and rolled behind al-Salah's SUV.

Al-Salah and Yassim bent down, grabbed the satchel at the same time, and began struggling for it.

Jamal grabbed Sara and pulled her down behind a busted up VW sedan.

Qadir jumped into the fray, knocking al-Salah down.

Yassim managed to pull free, the satchel now in his possession.

One of al-Salah's bodyguards let loose a torrent of rounds that struck Qadir who fell to the ground clutching his abdomen.

Jamal discharged another burst of rounds, this time killing the one guard who had shot Qadir.

Al-Salah's other guard grabbed and pulled him back from the scene behind the van Sara had arrived in. He shielded al-Salah from the line of fire.

Al-Hakim, Attlee and the boys dropped behind the Rover.

Hamed gripped his AK and jumped behind Yassim's sedan. He fired at Yassim who darted over to Burns.

Yassim was not hit. His driver ducked down beside him too.

"I only want my daughter and I'm out of here," Burns said to Yassim. "You can stay and fight over this *ḥadīth*."

Yassim nodded breathlessly.

"We had an agreement," al-Salah shouted to Yassim.

"You know this *ḥadīth* belongs to the Brotherhood, for Bakr was the true one!" Yassim yelled. "A'isha wrote this."

"You want to conceal the truth it was A'isha who was wrong all along," al-Salah said. "Ali was the chosen one."

Jamal, on the ground beside Sara, squinted at her. She looked back at him.

"Jamal!" Burns hollered from his position next to Yassim. "I'm walking out of here with my daughter, your niece. You understand?"

"I am willing to die for Allah if he commands it. I will kill her as I killed her mother, for Allah had commanded it."

Burns exhaled in frustration and surveyed the standoff.

Sara, who understood Arabic because she had studied it for her foreign language undergraduate component in college, said in Arabic, "You are my uncle?"

He did not answer her.

"What does my father mean you killed my mother?"

Again, he did not answer. She shook his shoulder and said, "You are my mother's brother? And you killed her? Why?"

He turned and slapped her across the face. "Be still, woman!"

She smarted from the slap, rubbing her cheek. Looking around, she grabbed a rock, the size of her hand, and whacked him on the back of his head. He dropped his rifle and grasped his head using both of his hands.

She grabbed the rifle, held it on him and stood, backing up.

Burns jumped up from behind the Mercedes, his hands in the air. "Listen everyone. We're walking out of here. All of you can stay and fight over this *ḥadīth*. That does not matter to us."

"Did he really kill Mother?" She had an edge in her voice as she glanced back at Burns.

"Yes," he said, moving closer. "He is your uncle and he killed the only woman I ever loved, your mother. An honor killing. I am sorry for not telling you the truth."

She kept backing up towards her father. Jamal rubbed his sore head, blood oozing from the wound. He stood and stumbled towards her.

"Sara!" Burns shouted.

"Stop!" she said, leveling the AK at Jamal.

Jamal hesitated, stopping briefly, but then crept toward her again. She continued to back away from him.

"Jamal," Burns said. "Don't do anything stupid."

"What I do is commanded by Allah himself!" he said, his face contorted.

"Man is responsible for his actions," Sara said. "Allah does not command man to kill man."

"Shut up, stupid woman. You know not what you say." He continued to edge towards her.

"The *Qur'an* says," she continued, " 'nor slay the soul Allah has forbidden.' That means mankind."

Jamal kept edging towards her, his face taut.

Burns approached from behind Sara slowly, cautiously.

"So why would you disobey Allah?" She said to Jamal.

Jamal said nothing.

"I asked you a question," she said.

"I do not answer to women!" He lunged for her.

She squeezed the trigger. An eruption of bullets from the AK sprayed the ground near Jamal's feet, dirt kicking up onto him. He flinched and stopped in his tracks.

"Answer me!" she yelled, tears now streaming down her face.

"Your whore mother slept with this infidel, and Allah ordered me to kill her for dishonoring her family and disobeying Allah's will."

"Allah does not tell anyone to kill his children," she said, shaking.

"And now, he has commanded me to kill you too." He unsheathed a *jambiya* from under his belt and lunged for her, the knife high in the air over his head.

She closed her eyes tightly and squeezed the trigger. The kick from the rifle knocked her backwards and onto the ground.

Jamal went down full of bullets.

Burns made a dash for Sara, grabbing her and diving behind the banged up VW sedan. From their vantage point, they saw Jamal was still alive, but barely.

Yassim made a dash to his car.

Hamed opened fire on Yassim. Yassim was not hit, but managed to duck behind the back of his sedan. His driver stayed close to him.

Qadir, who had been hit earlier, rose slightly to fire on Hamed striking him. Hamed collapsed dead near al-Salah.

Jamal stared at Burns, his eyes aflame. Unable to move, he coughed up blood.

"Allah has thus decided your fate, Jamal," Burns said, looking back at him.

Jamal, his face contorted in horror, quivered violently, then expired.

Chapter Thirty-Eight

Several rounds from an unknown Uzi sprayed al-Salah's surviving bodyguard. He fell dead next to Qadir, who finally succumbed to his wounds.

A volley of rounds then struck Yassim's driver. He hunched over dead.

Major Garrett and his three black-ops men appeared from around the side of the house. One of the black-ops men subdued al-Salah and another Yassim. Garrett took possession of the satchel from Yassim.

The third black-ops man secured the weapon Sara had used.

"It's over, Sergeant Burns," Garrett said in English. "Do me a favor and collect those weapons." He waved his Uzi over the scene.

Burns promptly picked up all of the weapons in the area. One of the black-ops men then collected the weapons from him. Everyone gathered in the center of the yard, except one black-ops man who tossed all the weapons into their Humvee parked around the other side of the house.

"That belongs to the Brotherhood of Bakr," Yassim said, looking at the satchel in Garrett's hand.

"It is for all Muslims," al-Salah said.

"Perhaps," Garrett said in Arabic. "And I saw how well you cooperated in that matter." He looked over at Burns who now held Sara close. "You need to load up, Professor, and follow us. The Saudis will not let you leave once they get wind of this."

Burns and Sara hurried over to the Rover and climbed in.

Al-Hakim, Attlee and the students mounted up after them.

Garrett signaled to his men to move out. They retreated around the corner of the house to the parked Humvee.

"You are letting us live?" Yassim said.

"Yeah, well, we all need enemies," Garrett said.

The Humvee pulled around in front of the house. Garrett jumped in and said, just before closing the door, "Who's going to believe this crazy story anyway?"

The Humvee sped away followed by the Rover.

Yassim and al-Salah stood there, weaponless, without the *ḥadīth*, disbelieving that the Americans had let them live.

Chapter Thirty-Nine

In Baghdad Burns and Sara flew out on a military transport. They took a bus from Ramstein Air Base to Frankfurt where they booked a civilian flight to New Orleans. There, they spent a couple days together. Sara texted Jennifer in Paris the news she was all right and back in the States with her father.

Sitting at Café Du Monde in the French Quarter, Burns handed Sara A'isha's necklace. "I want you to have this."

She took it and said, "What is it?"

Burns smiled. "A very famous and courageous lady once owned that."

She examined it. "It looks like it belongs in a museum."

Burns chuckled. "Perhaps. But I want you to keep it safe and hand it down to your female descendants." He took it back from her and placed it over her head where it came to rest against her chest.

Sara squinted at him.

He squeezed her hand and said, "I'll explain it all someday."

A couple days later on his way back to Iraq, Burns stopped in

London and met up with al-Hakim at the University of Cambridge. Al-Hakim had printed up the photographs of the *ḥadīth*, and had already separated and cataloged them.

"Well, we do have the photographs, Patrick. I will duplicate and enhance them and present them to the university with a full accounting."

"Yeah, but this will not be accepted without the originals," Burns said.

"I know." Al-Hakim shifted in his chair. "The only way to introduce this to the scholarly world for acceptance is to have access to the *ḥadīth*. That is the only way it can be authenticated and attributed to A'isha."

"That, Ahmed, may be impossible to do."

Colonel Graves, dressed in a civilian suit and tie, walked into the main entrance to the Central Intelligence Agency in Langley, Virginia carrying Burns' satchel.

Inside, he met up with an older man who carried an empty documents-storage box. Graves followed him down a hallway to a large, temperature-controlled room. The man entered a code into the system and a heavily vaulted door slowly swung open. He stepped into the room, Graves following. The door closed behind them.

The room contained thousands of document-storage boxes. Graves followed the man down a row between two shelves of storage boxes.

The man put on reading glasses he had dangling around his neck. He scanned a few storage boxes on a shelf then stopped next to one in particular. "Here," he said, handing Graves the empty documents-storage box.

Graves took the codices out of the satchel and placed them in the documents-storage box. He closed the box.

The man placed the box on the shelf next to another. He scribbled a number on the side of the box and cataloged it on a slip of paper he held.

Graves noticed the box next to the one he had placed the codices in was entitled: *Lance of Longinus.*

Longinus was the name of the Roman soldier who had pierced

Jesus' side as he hung on the cross in John's account of the Crucifixion. The *Lance of Longinus* was the spear he had used.
    The two men departed.

The End

About the Author
s.milsap.thorpe@gmail.com

Mr. Thorpe works for an international agency extensively throughout the Middle East.

***VISIT OUR WEBSITE
FOR THE FULL INVENTORY
OF QUALITY BOOKS*:**

http://www.roguephoenixpress.com

Rogue Phoenix Press
Representing Excellence in Publishing

*Quality trade paperbacks and downloads
in multiple formats,
in genres ranging from historical to contemporary romance, mystery and
science fiction.
Visit the website then bookmark it.
We add new titles each month!*

Made in the USA
Charleston, SC
25 June 2016